T0113590

# Not You AGAIN

Lanelle Thomas

# Not You AGAIN

ARCHWAY
PUBLISHING

This is a work of fiction. All of the characters, names, incidents, organizations, and dialogue in this novel are either the products of the author's imagination or are used fictitiously.

Archway Publishing books may be ordered through booksellers or by contacting:

Archway Publishing
1663 Liberty Drive
Bloomington, IN 47403
www.archwaypublishing.com
844-669-3957

Cover design by Celeste Swing.

Map illustration by Brandon Sorenson.

ISBN: 978-1-6657-1762-5 (sc)
ISBN: 978-1-6657-1763-2 (e)

Library of Congress Control Number: 2022900509

Print information available on the last page.

Archway Publishing rev. date: 2/10/2022

To Bo – the man who loves me despite all my orneriness and stubbornness. I love you.

Land of Uspia

Aspil

Estar

Uspon

Athein

Loshia

# Chapter 1

"And now, for a special presentation from the Royal Family!"

The announcement the television makes draws the attention of my whole family from various parts of the house. We gather around to hear what they have to share.

"Good morning, good people of Uspia," greets King Harden. He is a tall, broad man with a full head of salt and pepper hair and a short beard to match. His blue eyes pierce through the camera. "As you all know, my son, Prince Zane, is turning twenty-one in a couple of days. This means that he has come to the age where he needs to choose a wife and prepare to take my place as king."

My eyes narrow and my head turns to the side, waiting for his next words.

"Queen Gabrielle, Prince Zane, and I are pleased to invite all of the eldest daughters of our leading province families to Uspon for the next month, to vie for the prince's hand!"

My mouth drops open as the camera zooms to prince Zane's face where he looks into the camera and gives a dazzling smile. He has dirty blonde hair and the same piercing blue eyes as his father.

My mom, dad, and sister all turn to me with excitement in their eyes. My little sister breaks the short silence with a loud squeal.

I rub my ears. "Dang, Violet!"

"I'm sorry! I'm just so excited!" she proclaims, jumping up and down in her spot.

I look to mom and dad and try to gauge their feelings about it. Mom's eyes show the same excitement as Violet's, while dad's show what seems to be a mixture of excitement and worry.

The king continues, "We would like all the eligible ladies to be in Uspon by the end of the day. We will be starting things off, tomorrow night, with a ball! We cannot wait to see all of you!" The broadcast ends.

Violet lets out another squeal.

"Hush, honey!" My mom directs at her. She looks at me. "Well, this is an exciting announcement! What do you think?"

I take in a deep breath. "I don't really know what to think." My thoughts are spinning around me.

"Well, I think it's exciting," pipes in Violet.

"Really?" I ask her, sarcastically. "I don't think any of us got that impression with your squealing."

She sticks her tongue at me, and I roll my eyes.

"Girls," my father warns.

I walk over to the floor-to-ceiling and wall-to-wall window that overlooks the province my parents take care of. I watch as the sky dumps another layer of the white stuff down on the city. Snow never goes away in the province of Aspil. I love the snow, but sometimes I wish I could be under a warm sun, tanning my very porcelain skin.

Part of me is excited because I get to be wooed by a prince. I mean, this is the stuff of fairytales. But life isn't a fairytale, and he could be a complete jerk off.

"Penny for your thoughts?" My dad asks as he joins me at the window.

"Four things could happen: He is wonderful and chooses me, he is awful and sends me home, he is awful and chooses me, or —" I take a breath, "he is wonderful and sends me home."

He grunts in agreement.

I look up at him. "Is it worth it?"

He turns around and glances at mom. "It is." He smiles.

Dad and mom are the fairytale that everyone wants. Not like the ones in movies, but the real ones. There is attraction and laughter, but there are also hardships, which they get through together. They have grown closer and stronger throughout the years. I want that.

"I'll go pack my bags." I smile at my dad, turn around, and make my way up the stairs.

I open my large walk-in closet and stare at my clothes, wondering what in the world I need to wear at the castle for the next month.

The King mentioned that everything will kick off with a ball, so I pick out my favorite gown. It is a silky, form fitting, strapless, royal blue gown, that ends in a mermaid flare at the bottom.

*But how many balls are going to happen?*

I pick out two more dresses and add them to my garment bag with the first.

Heaven only knows what kinds of things we will need to do to impress the prince while we are there, so I pick out a few pant suits and casual outfits. I add a workout outfit, pajamas, shoes, and make-up and head out the bedroom with my bags.

"Let me take these, miss," one of our servants says as they relieve me of my load.

"Thank you."

I stop at the full-length hall mirror and look myself over. I am a tall girl with an hourglass shape. I have platinum blonde hair that falls to the bottom of my shoulder blades. I have brown eyes that contrast my light hair and skin. I wonder what the other girls look like? Will I even have a chance?

"Char?" My mom calls from downstairs.

"Coming!"

When I get downstairs, I see my family and our servants gathered, waiting for me. I pause, my eyes widening.

Violet is bopping up and down in her spot, keeping the squealing inside. My mom stands next to her with a big smile and tears in her eyes. My dad stands next to her in his quiet, stoic manner.

"What?" I ask.

My mom rushes over and gives me a hug. "I am going to miss you so much." She sniffles.

I wrap my arms around her. A month is the longest that I have ever been gone from home. "I'll be back before you know it."

She pulls back and lets my dad approach.

We wrap each other in a hug, and he says, "Stay you. Either he falls for you or he doesn't, but don't change who you are."

We pull apart. "I won't." I smile.

I walk over to my sister and put my hands on her shoulders to stop her from bouncing before I give her a hug.

"Give me updates with lots of details!" She giggles.

I roll my eyes, smiling. "I will."

I pull away from her and look around the room one last time. I take a deep breath, smile, and head towards the waiting car that will drive me to Uspon, my home for the next month.

⚜

After a few hours of driving through Aspil's snow, we enter the more temperate climate of Uspon. It's May, so the further we drive into Uspon, the more green and sunshine we see.

I look at the dashboard and see it shows that the temperature outside is seventy degrees. I roll down my window and feel it for myself. Feeling the warmth on my skin makes goose bumps appear. We only leave Aspil once a year for a family trip, and when we do, it's on a plane to enjoy Athein's beaches in the summer. I have never felt such a perfect temperature before today.

I must have enjoyed myself a little too much, because the next thing I know I am waking up to my driver saying, "We are here, miss."

After a good stretch, I step out of the car. I take my bags from my driver and head up the marble stairs to the front entrance. I only make it halfway up when a tall woman wearing a black dress that hugs her pencil thin body, appears with a clipboard in her hands. She has coal-black hair pulled into a tight bun and doesn't look very friendly.

"Hello." I greet with a smile.

She looks up from her clipboard, raises an eyebrow, and asks, "Name?"

"Chartreuse Moore from Aspil, ma'am."

"Follow me." Her about-face was rather impressive considering the six-inch heels she is wearing.

I follow her into the castle to a foyer with a red carpet covering the marble floor and a crystal chandelier hanging from a painted ceiling of the sky. Directly in front of me is a large staircase where the red carpet continues up and divides into two smaller staircases a little way up, going in opposite directions.

She leads me up the stairs and to the left. "This is the wing where you ladies will be staying."

She stops at a door at the end of the hall and opens it. "This is your room. The Prince is busy for the rest of the day, but you will all be dining with him tomorrow night. Take tonight to get acquainted with the castle."

I thank her as I walk into my room. "Wait! What is your ..." She shuts the door. "Name?"

I audibly exhale and look around my room.

Directly across from me are glass double doors that lead out to a large marble balcony. To my right is a king-sized, four-post bed, a chaise, and the bathroom. An ornate vanity and a walk-in closet are to my left.

I put my bags along the wall and head out onto the balcony. There is a tiny table and two chairs in the corner. Out past the balcony is a spacious, green garden with a simple hedge maze and benches that are sprinkled throughout with a large fountain in the middle. I can't help but smile. *That* is where I want to be.

I leave my room and find my way to the garden. It smells like they have just mowed. I start walking through the maze. The towering greenery are rose bushes of varying shades. It makes the garden incredibly fragrant.

I make it to the far side of the garden where a tall, metal fence protects the grounds. I gaze through it and look into the dense forest that lays slightly beyond it.

Just then a strong breeze comes through and blows my sheer scarf off my neck. I try to catch it but am unsuccessful. Thankfully, one of the spikes at the top of the fence grabs hold of it.

I let out a sigh of relief. I put my feet on the bottom of the fence and stretch as high as I can to reach my scarf. I end up having to stand on my toes before I can feel the gentle fabric between my fingers.

*Gotcha.*

I get ready to lower myself back to the ground when someone grabs me from behind, wrapping their arms around mine. I let out a yell.

Once my feet touch the ground, I stomp my heel onto their foot, followed by slamming my head into their face. They release me and fall to the ground. I turn around and get myself into a fighting stance. One of the palace guards looks up at me through his hands, tears in his eyes.

"What did you do that for?!" He asks, pained.

*Oops.*

"What did you grab me for?!"

"You were climbing the fence! It looked suspicious!"

"I was grabbing my scarf." I roll my eyes, placing it back around my neck.

He pulls his hands back to check for blood. "You could have broken my nose!"

"But I didn't!"

He stands up and glares at me. I glare back.

"Let me guess. One of the girls here for Zane?"

I straighten myself. "Yes."

"And which province are you from?"

"Aspil."

"Well, suspicious fence climber from Aspil ..."

"I have a name."

"What is it?" he asks, annoyed.

"Chartreuse Moore."

"Well, Miss Moore, try not to climb anymore fences during your stay."

I narrow my eyes at him. "I didn't do it for fun."

He shrugs. "If you need assistance next time one of your garments gets caught on a fence ..." He nods towards the fence. "Come get one of us." He turns around and starts to walk away.

I am fuming inside and cannot let him leave with the last word. "If I do need help, I am not coming to you, that's for sure!" I yell.

He gives a dismissive wave without turning around and disappears into the maze.

I let out a groan. What a frustrating man. I hope I don't have to see much of him while I am here.

⁘

After the fence encounter, I decide to take my dinner in my room. The castle staff serves me moist, roast chicken with steamed vegetables, fresh baked bread, and lemon water.

As I am in the middle of eating my dinner, I hear an agitated female voice coming from the hall. I press my ear to the door.

"Oh, do keep up! Ten bags are not that bad. My parents talked me down from the fifteen that I originally wanted to bring!"

*Fifteen bags?!*

I think about the three bags I brought and shake my head. I am curious to see what this girl looks like. I crack open my door and peek out into the hall. At the door to the room adjacent to mine is a tall, tan girl with hair so brown it's almost black. She stands, playing on her phone, while her servant clearly struggles to get her bags into the room. I shake my head.

I back up and shut my door quietly. Judging by the way her skin is blessed by the sun, I am guessing she comes from either the mediterranean province of Athein or the arid province of Estar. I guess I will find out tomorrow.

I finish my dinner and then crawl into bed. My body sinks into the mattress while the soft, fluffy blankets surround me. It doesn't take me long to fall asleep.

# Chapter 2

I am woken up by a light tapping on my door.

I groan. "Come in."

"It is time for breakfast with the other ladies, miss." A short and petite servant informs me.

"Thank you. I will be down in just a few minutes."

She gives me a small nod and shuts the door.

*What time is it?*

I turn and look at the clock on the wall.

*Seven?!* I guess we won't be sleeping in while we're here.

I get out of bed and head over to the vanity. I am not too concerned with my appearance since the prince will not be there, so I just brush my hair, throw on my slippers, and head downstairs.

When I get down to the dining room, two other girls are already there, neither of which are the girl from last night. One is the same tan color as the girl from the hall, but instead of being smooth, it is a little rough, like leather. Her hair is a lovely chestnut brown. My guess is she is the girl from Estar.

The other girl, I am assuming from the providence of Loshia, has flawless black skin with smooth, wavy black hair. She looks up from her spot at the table and smiles at me. She seems kind. After I get my breakfast, I take the seat next to her.

"Hi, I am Chartreuse from Aspil." I hold out my hand.

She shakes it and replies with, "Hi. Kya from Loshia," in a thick accent.

*One out of three.*

We turn to our plates and begin to eat. The other girl sits down across from Kya.

"Hi! I am Chartreuse from Aspil. What's your name?"

She barely meets my eyes and says, "Jazzie."

I let out a quiet sigh and am about to get back to my breakfast when a loud, feminine giggle echoes into the room from the hall. It sounds like the girl from last night.

She glides into the room, her sheer, feather robe, swirling around her feet.

"Hello ladies!" She exclaims with a sickeningly fake smile on her face. I politely smile back.

She floats over to the table filled with food, grabs a grapefruit, and takes the seat across from me.

"Hi! I am Daphne!" She holds her hand over the table to me, her feathery sleeve almost touching my food. I look at her sleeve, then her.

She looks at her arm. "Oh! I am sorry! It is hard to avoid such a big plate of food."

*Oh ho ho.*

I narrow my eyes at her.

Obviously pleased with herself, she turns her attention to her breakfast.

We all eat in awkward silence for a few minutes when the tall woman who greeted me at the castle doors yesterday, walks into the room.

"Good morning ladies," she greets with an uninterested edge.

"Good morning," we all answer in unison.

"My name is Ms. Maren and I am going to basically be your dame while you are. I will be keeping you in line while you all attempt to impress His Highness. My job, is to make sure you do not make a mockery of your families, or our country."

*Dang.*

We all go tense.

Ms. Maren must be pleased with this because I see a barely noticeable smile creep across her lips.

"After you have finished your breakfast, change into appropriate clothing for horseback riding. Meet me on the front steps when you are done." She does that impressive about-face again and leaves.

Daphne gets up out of her seat. "Well, I am stuffed."

I look down at her half-eaten grapefruit and raise my eyebrows at her.

"I will see you ladies out there!" She glides out of the room.

The tension immediately eases with both of their departures. The rest of us finish our breakfast in peace.

✦

I am glancing through my closet for something to wear to go horseback riding. I imagine some of the girls will have actual horse-riding gear. I, however, have nothing. I have never ridden a horse before.

*Great. My first activity as a girl vying for the prince is going to be a complete failure.*

I settle on my jeans, a long-sleeve shirt with thumb holes, and my black boots. I throw my hair into a ponytail and head towards the castle's front steps.

I am not the first girl there. I am also not the last. Daphne is missing, no doubt trying to make her appearance a special one. The prince isn't even here. I roll my eyes to myself.

Jazzie is in riding gear. She gives me a quick once-over but doesn't say anything. Kya gives me a warm smile. I smile back.

She is wearing leggings, a loose long-sleeve shirt, and boots. I am glad I am not the only one in "unofficial gear."

A couple of minutes pass and Daphne finally shows up. She, of course, looks like she will be a pro on the horse. She has everything from the vest to the riding crop in her hand to the tight French braid pulling her hair back.

She gives me and Kya a glance and scoff before joining Jazzie.

Ms. Maren steps out from behind a bush making us jump.

"Punctuality is a must, Daphne," she says.

Daphne gives a shallow curtsy and replies, "Yes, ma'am."

"Follow me."

We all hurriedly fall in step behind her. She leads us to a beautiful white stable with gray doors and window shudders. I notice there is not the usual smells that accompany a stable; at least, all the ones I have ever been in. It is near spotless inside in the aisle. I feel pity for whoever has to keep it in this shape.

"Pick your companion, ladies," Ms. Maren commands.

We shuffle around, checking out the individual stalls. Everyone else claims their horse quickly. I am drawn to a skittish beauty in the stall furthest from where we came in. She peeks me at through her mane with sad eyes. I plant myself in front of her door, showing she is my choice.

"Good. Now, go in, mount your horses, and meet me outside."

When I open her door, she gives a little jump.

"Shh. It's ok girl." I slowly reach my hand out. She leans away from it, but once we connect, she leans into my hand. "That's it."

I run my hand across her back and find the saddle. I look at her to see how she is doing. She seems fine. I put my first foot in the stirrup and check again. Still good. I hop up and settle in, waiting for nervous movement from her when my weight rests on her back. Nothing. I breathe a sigh of relief. I give her a soft kick in the side while pulling her reins towards her door. She doesn't budge.

*Ah. Here is where you will give me trouble.*

I try again. Nothing. I rub her neck and whisper, "Come on, girl. You can do it."

Daphne scoffs as she trots by on her regal, midnight black horse.

"See? Like they are doing." I give her a slightly harder kick. She moves but she is all over the place.

"Whoa!" I have to yank her reins this way and that for a minute before she gets the concept.

This time, I am the last one. We pull up to the rest of the group.

"Having trouble, Miss Moore?" Ms. Maren asks.

"No ma'am. I believe we are all good now."

Boy was I wrong. Everyone else is able to follow Ms. Maren and her horse in a perfect straight line, while my horse and I are all over the path at the end of the line.

Suddenly, she darts off the path, finds herself a nice Black Hawthorne bush, and starts chowing down.

"Really?!" I try to nudge her back to the path. She isn't going anywhere. "You are one stubborn girl."

I let out a sign of frustration and look around. I can't even see everyone else now.

"Oh, come on! Really?!" I somewhat shout.

"What seems to be the problem ma' ...."

I turn towards the voice and see *him.*

"Ah. Miss Moore, was it?"

I purse my lips and level my eyes at him. "Mm-hm." I turn back to my horse.

"I see you grabbed Water Canyon. She is our most stubborn horse."

I look back at him. "You don't say." My voice is heavy with sarcasm.

He shrugs. "You guys are a perfect fit."

*Oh no he didn't.*

*He isn't totally wrong.*

"Don't you have more important duties to attend to, like, I don't know, guarding the prince?"

He gives me a smug smile. "I am. I am scouting the territory. He is following behind."

*Oh no.*

I see a horse and rider approach from behind Mr. Smug.

*Great. My first time meeting the prince and my stubborn horse won't move!*

I am frozen in place when he pulls up. He gives a big, white grin. I can't help but smile back.

"Good morning, miss. What is your name?"

"Chartreuse Moore, Your Highness." I give a small curtsy.

"Ah, from Aspil. It is a pleasure to meet you." He offers a bow in return.

"The pleasure is mine, Your Highness."

His guard raises an eyebrow at me. I squint my eyes at him. Prince Zane turns and looks at him.

"How rude of me. This is my personal bodyguard and friend, Reed."

"Nice to finally know your name, *Reed*." I give him a smirk.

"Oh! You two have met before?" Prince Zane's eyes are wide and looking between the two of us.

"Yes, Zane. This is the girl I told you about."

*What?*

*Oh no.*

I can feel my face heating up.

Reed is smirking at me, and Prince Zane is trying his hardest to stifle a grin.

"Don't be embarrassed, Miss Moore. I am quite impressed how you bested Reed."

I smile at this.

"She did not best me. She caught me off guard." He glares at his friend.

"You are a trained royal guard. You have been trained *not* to be." The prince is grinning back at him.

I hear horses and feminine giggles approaching from behind me.

"We should go, Your Highness, before you get mobbed by all of the girls," Reed warns.

Prince Zane sighs. "It's probably a good idea." He grabs my hand and plants a kiss on the back. "Until tonight then, Miss Moore."

I can only smile and nod.

Prince Zane and Reed take off back the way they came.

"Dear heavens, Miss Moore, we thought we lost you!" exclaimed Ms. Maren.

I just motioned my hand over my horse and her midmorning snack. The girls all giggle behind her. She quickly shushes them.

"Do you think that you can control your horse now, Miss Moore?"

I yank on Water Canyon's reins as hard as I can, and she finally snaps to attention. "Yes, ma'am."

"Good." She clicks to her horse and starts on back to the castle.

I fall in line behind the other girls and, thankfully, make it back without further incident.

⁂

I collapse onto my bed and try to shake away my forest fiasco. It wasn't bad enough that I embarrassed myself in front of Ms. Moore and the girls, but I had to run into *Reed* again and meet the prince that way! I am pretty sure if there is a scorecard of us ladies, I am dead last right now.

My rumbling stomach interrupts my angsting. I call down to the kitchen and ask for a simple lunch of a sandwich and water. Not five minutes later do I hear a knocking on my door.

"Come in!"

A servant sets my food down and disappears as quickly as she came in. I lift the lid to find my simple lunch, *not* so simple. My sandwich is six inches tall, stuffed with three different meats and cheeses accompanied by fresh vegetables, topped off with a toothpick and olive. My water is filled with various fruits bouncing on the bubbles making their way to the top.

*Geez.*

I am only able to make it about halfway through my lunch before I call it quits and crash on my bed.

⁂

"Miss? Miss?"

I startle straight up on my bed. "What?!" Seeing it's one of the servants, I take a relieved breath. "Sorry. Yes?"

"It is time to get ready for the ball, miss."

I whip my head around to the clock on the wall. *Holy crap! I napped for three hours?!*

"I have started your bath for you."

"Thank you." I follow her to the bathroom, undress, and climb into the bath. I sink into the hot, bubbly water, and lean against the back of the tub. She proceeds to wash my hair. I can't help but close my eyes. I am not the biggest fan of being waited on, especially when it's something I can do myself, but this is one thing that I gladly let others do for me.

When she finishes, I wash the rest of myself and meet her in the closet. I point to the first dress that I packed. We get me squeezed into it and head over to the vanity. I get nervous with pointy objects by my eyes, so I do my own make up. I put on a light layer of foundation, a tender pink shade to my lips, mascara, and give my eyes a smoky finish.

As my servant starts on my hair, I realize that I do not know her name yet.

"What is your name?"

She seems taken aback. "Oh! It's Elise, miss."

"That's a beautiful name." I smile.

She tries to hide her smile. "Thank you, miss."

"You're welcome."

She sprays my hair to keep it into place. She has put it into a loose messy bun with curly tendrils framing my face. I love it.

"This is beautiful, Elise. Thank you."

She gives me a big smile. "You're welcome, miss."

I add a pair of dangling diamond earrings to finish off the look. I walk over to the full-length mirror and look myself over. I feel beautiful. I only hope this confidence lasts when I see the other girls.

I throw on my shiny, black flats, leave my room, and head towards to ballroom. As I round the railing, nerve-inducing chatter fills my ears. I stand at the top and gaze over the crowd of people that are littered around the first floor. They can't possibly match the number of people in the ballroom. I take a deep breath and begin my descent. A few faces look towards me, and my hands begin to sweat. More faces turn towards me, and my grip tightens on the railing. I reach the bottom, give them all a polite smile, and make my way to the ballroom.

I was right, *a lot* more people await inside. A guard stands at the entrance and asks how I would like to be introduced.

"Oh, could you not introduce me, please?"

He raises an eyebrow at me. "My lady, you are one of the guests of honor, I am required to introduce you."

I grimace and groan. "Chartreuse Moore of Aspil." I look down.

He bangs his staff on the ground two times, making me jump. "Introducing Lady Chartreuse Moore of Aspil."

I make my way in to smiles and chattering. I put on my best smile and nod every few people. When I finally reach a corner, I swipe a glass of champagne and down it.

"Going to be one of the drunks, huh?"

I spin around and find none other than *Reed.*

I roll my eyes. "What do you want?"

"I am making my rounds and greeting all of the visiting ladies. It's the *polite* thing to do."

I doubt this man know anything about polite.

I peek and see him looking me from head to toe.

"You clean up well."

I snort. "Uh, thanks?"

He shrugs off my attitude. "That's a compliment from me, take it or leave it."

I sigh. "Fine. Thank you."

"You're welcome."

Two more bangs sound the room. "Introducing Lady Daphne Starling from Athein."

*Of course her last name would be something like that.* I subtly shake my head.

I hear oo's and ah's from around the room. When Daphne comes into view, I see why. Her beautiful skin is nothing short of exposed in a strappy dress that loops around her neck, hangs low in the front, showing off her gifted bosom, and connects to her micro-mini skirt with only a gold ring on the front and back. The turquoise fabric compliments her tan skin.

And there goes some of my confidence.

"Well, I best be off. Have a good evening, Miss Moore." Reed gives me a bow and makes his way to Daphne. I grab another glass and take a big sip.

Thankfully, Kya was the next girl in, and I quickly plant myself next to her. She is wearing a royal purple, satin gown that goes all the way to the floor with a sweetheart neckline. She is stunning. Jazzie is the last to enter a few minutes later. She wears a lovely cream colored cocktail dress that compliments her darker skin.

Trumpets announce the entrance of the Royal Family. King Harden is the first to enter, followed by Queen Gabriella, and lastly, Prince Zane. He looks handsome in his black tuxedo.

Once they reach their dais, they turn and face us.

"Good evening and welcome! We are very pleased to have everyone here and we hope you are all enjoying yourselves. To our four very special guests, Prince Zane will take turns dancing with each one of you throughout the night." King Harden smiles at us. Giggles erupt around the room. I feel myself smile and look around at the other girls. Daphne is flirtatiously looking at Prince Zane, Kya is bashfully peeking up at him, while Jazzie's expression is the only one I have seen so far, stoic, and somewhat uninterested.

The music starts back up and everyone quickly makes a large circle in the middle of the floor. Prince Zane steps down from the dais and makes his way to the circle. He approaches Daphne first. They give everyone a graceful performance. He chooses Jazzie next. You can tell he is trying to be friendly, but she is stiff in his arms with her usual expression the whole time. Kya is his next choice. They seem very comfortable with each other.

Finally, he approaches me. I wipe my sweaty hands on my dress before grabbing hold of his hand and going to the middle of the floor.

We start our turn. Thankfully, I know how to dance and can keep up with him.

"It is good to see you again, Lady Moore." He gives me one of his glowing smiles.

"Thank you. It's good to see you again too, Prince Zane.

Although, would you mind just calling me Chartreuse from now on. Lady just sounds weird to me."

He chuckles. "Absolutely. Could you extend me the same courtesy and just call me Zane?"

I smile. "Will do."

"Have you enjoyed your time here so far?"

I think about everything that has happened. The good, like meeting Kya. The bad, like meeting Reed. I must have hesitated too long.

"Uh oh."

"No! I have had a great time — mostly."

"What has made it only a 'mostly'?"

"There is this guard …"

"Reed?"

"How did you know?!"

"He tends to rub people the wrong way. After hearing about your guy's first encounter and how you guys ran into each other again, I put two and two together." He grins.

I sigh. "I am sorry. I know he's your friend."

He shrugs. "It's ok! I still love him." He leans closer to me and whispers, "Although, I may be the only one."

We chuckle.

After a spin out, our song ends. He kisses my hand and I bow back.

I make my way out of the ballroom and to the stairs. I did my part and danced with the prince. I was done for the night. I am *not* a fan of mingling with hordes of strangers.

As I begin climbing, I feel like I am being watched. I glance around. I don't see anyone until I am almost to the top. At the entrance of the ballroom, is Reed, who promptly looks away.

# Chapter 3

Yesterday, the day after the ball, was uneventful, except for the bomb drop of an announcement that the Royal Family and all of us ladies were going to be making visits to all our provinces to meet our families and show what each province has to offer. So, here I am packing again.

When I get down to the castle's courtyard, I see three limos waiting. One is reserved for the royal family and two for us ladies. I choose the limo that doesn't have Daphne shoving in four bags into the trunk. I put my bag in the back, open the door, and see my ride to the airport is: Jazzie.

*This is going to be an awkward drive.*

I get in and give her a small, friendly smile. I am met with a stare, though not as cold as usual, before she stares out the window.

*Progress!*

The driver gets a call in his earpiece, and we are off.

I decide to press my luck with Jazzie. "So, I have never been to Estar. How is it?"

"Hot."

A particular phrase that involves a swear and a detective comes to my mind. "Of course. I meant, what kind of crops, animals, or goods do you guys have?"

Seeing that I am not going to let this be a silent drive, she gives in. "We grow a lot of herbs and spices, like basil, chamomile, and lemon balm."

"I am assuming you have camels?"

"Yes, and foxes, coyotes, snakes, and lizards."

"Do you like living there?"

"Usually. However, it has been a particularly bad year, so crops have been poorer, which means our income has dwindled, making things hard." Her voice is filled with emotion.

"I am sorry."

"And our 'lovely' Royal Family has done nothing to help us." Anger replaces the earlier sadness.

"Are they aware of Estar's troubles?"

"Of course, they are. I am sure they have noticed a change in their perfectly seasoned poultry." She goes back to looking out the window.

I feel bad for her and her people. I don't know how, but I want to help. Does the Royal Family know? If so, why haven't they aided Estar?

We pull into the airport, in front of a private jet. Everyone files out of their limos. The Royal Family boards while us girls take our luggage to the cargo hold.

When it's my turn, I see it is no other than Reed loading the luggage in. I halt and glare.

He sees I am next, straightens up, and raises an eyebrow at me. He looks to my hands and asks, "That's all you have?"

"Yeah? Got a problem with that?"

"Not at all. All these other chicks brought at least three bags each. It's nice to have a smaller load." He takes my suitcase from me.

"What can I say, I am a simple girl."

He just stares at me.

*Awkward moment.*

I side-step and head onto the plane.

Once everyone is boarded, we are told that our first stop will be Loshia, followed by Athein, then Estar, and finally Aspil.

I settle into my seat, pulling out a book for our upcoming two-hour flight.

I bring out my noise cancelling headphones and put them on. I quickly get lost in my book.

⚜

The captain announces our arrival to Loshia. The second I step out of the fuselage and onto the plane's staircase, I am met with a wall of hot, humid air.

*Whew!*

I am not a fan of humidity, and it seems Loshia has it in spades.

There is a throng of reporters along the outskirts of the airport, snapping pictures. Zane and his parents smile and wave, as does Daphne. I just roll my eyes.

We all file into the limos in the same order as we did back in Uspon, and take off for Kya's home. I turn all the vents on my side of the car to me and soak in the cool, dry air.

We drive to a more secluded part of the island. Once we pass through a security gate, we pull up to one of the most beautiful homes I have ever seen. It has a sleek, modern look with sharp angles, metal railings, and lots of glass, showing us the interior of the main areas of the house. Unlike my house, which has a steep roof, Kya's is completely flat, allowing for a rooftop garden.

We are greeted by a warm, smiling couple, surrounded by several children of different ages.

"Hello! Welcome to Loshia, and our home." Kya's father greets. "I am Haku, this is my wife Likeke, and these are the rest of our children: Kaisa, Kincaid, Kalea, Kenna, and Kulani." He points to the person with the corresponding name.

I chuckle. The theme for their kids' names is the letter K like my parents stuck with the theme of naming my sister and I after colors. It's cute.

After Kya's mom tells us where to find our rooms, we all separate and unpack.

They gave me a room with an ocean view. I go out onto my personal balcony and enjoy the light mist rolling off the waves onto me. I love how close we are to the ocean. I can enjoy the sounds and smell of it in privacy.

I hunker down onto my chaise and get lost in my book again.

A few chapters later, I hear a knock at my door. I open it to find Zane.

"Oh! Zane! Hello."

"Hello, Chartreuse! I was wondering if you would like to accompany me on a drive to the local farmer's market?"

I smile. "I would love to."

When we get down to the limo, he opens my door for me.

"Such a gentleman." I straighten up and say playfully. "Thank you," I finish, seriously.

He gives me a little bow. "Anything, my lady." I catch a smirk as he shuts my door.

He joins me in the back seat and tells the driver our destination.

"So. You're my first date."

I snap my head his direction. "Out of all of us ladies?"

He shakes his head.

"*Ever?!*"

He nods his head, nervously.

"Wow. I would have thought that being the Prince kept you busy with the ladies."

"Oh, it does, at parties, with tons of people of around, but we are never alone."

"Well, thank you for choosing me as your first. I am honored." I give him a warm smile.

He returns it. "Good."

We pull up to a large street filled with vendors and their tents.

We step out and the smell of cooked meats, pastries, and spices fill the air. My stomach growls. I didn't realize how hungry I was.

"Shall we?" Zane asks, as he holds his elbow out to me.

I gladly wrapped my arm through his and we start our browsing.

"Anything in particular catching your attention?" He asks me.

I take in a deep breath. "Everything."

He chuckles.

I am not a fan of uncooked fish, so we passed by the vendors that offered such dishes. I finally pull us over to one where the meat is cooked.

They offer us a plate of rice that sits beneath a hamburger patty, egg, and brown gravy. Zane asks for two. We learn that the dish is called "Loco Moco."

It is delicious.

Zane breaks the silence as we stand in the street, eating. "What is your favorite type of meat?"

Without hesitation, I reply, "Hands down, beef. You?"

"I, myself, am a fan of pork."

"Pork *is* good. It's even better when combined with beef." I smile.

He chuckles. "That sounds like the kind of food Reed likes."

A small nod is all I offer to acknowledge his friend's name.

We finish our plates.

"Dessert?" He holds out his elbow again.

"Absolutely." I take it again.

I could stop at every single one of the dessert vendors, especially those that offer anything with chocolate. Since he was kind enough to let me pick the main dish, I ask which dessert is catching his eye. He pulls us over to the one that is offering what looks like a round, puffy croissant covered in powdered sugar.

We learn that it is called a "croissada" and is a fusion of a croissant and malasada. It's a perfect combination of light and flaky on the outside with a doughy inside. We like it so much that Zane orders us three servings of it.

Once we are finally full, he leads us to a bench at the edge of the beach. We sit down.

We gaze out across the vast ocean before us.

I am the one to break the silence. "Beautiful, isn't it?"

"Very. It is so peaceful here."

"Yes, it is."

"Is it peaceful in Aspil?"

"It is, but in a different way. Here, there are peaceful sounds, like the ocean waves. In Aspil, the snow deadens sound, so I am around peaceful silence."

"I can't wait to hear it, or *not* hear it."

I snort and we both start laughing.

We spend the rest of our time at the beach in peaceful silence.

⊱❄⊰

Zane drops me back off at my door, kisses my hand, and leaves. I am about to close my door when …

"Enjoy your date with Zane?"

I jump and peer into the hall to see Reed, leaning casually against my outside wall.

"As a matter of fact, I did."

"What did you guys do?"

I am about to tell him about our date when I remember who I am talking to.

"*That* is none of your business."

He raises an eyebrow at me.

"If you are that curious, you can just go ask your friend."

"I could, but this is more fun."

"What is?"

"Ticking you off."

I narrow my eyes at him and as I go back in to shut my door, I hear him chuckle.

*Jerk.*

<hr />

A few hours later is dinner. We all make our way to their large dining room. The walls are painted a light blue to mimic the color of the ocean. On the glass table are vases of white gardenia and plumeria.

There are white name cards placed around the table. Everyone slowly starts finding their seats. I am one of the last people standing up. I look further down the table and see Reed leaning back in his chair, with a huge, ornery grin on his face, holding a name card.

*Oh no.*

I walk over to him and snatch the card out of his hand. I look down to find my name.

I glare at him as I take my spot next to him.

I can smell the meat before they even bring the food out to us. They place large, shredded chunks of meat, wrapped up in some kind of leaf, in front of us. We learn this is a dish called "lau lau," that the meat is pork, and the leaves are taro.

Then they place down what looks like an upside-down strawberry cheesecake in a glass. I take a sip and am met with a glorious burst of strawberry and coconut.

I groan my approval.

"It's called 'lava flow'." Reed leans over and says to me.

I inspect the glass and, sure enough, the strawberry looks like lava flowing around in the coconut.

"Hm, that's cool."

"Yeah, it's a nice little drink."

Throughout dinner, Kya's parents teach us all about their island's crops. Apparently, all of Uspia's sugar cane and pineapples come from Loshia. They also farm many other things like coffee, avocados, beans, and potatoes.

Dinner is followed by — malasada. I look up at Zane and see him looking at me too. We both smile and look down.

I am somehow able to fit more of those fluffy little pastries down.

After everyone is done indulging in dessert, Kya stands up to address us.

"We would like to invite everyone to join us in one of our favorite activities as a family: nighttime manta ray snorkeling."

Several ooo's erupt from around the table. I, too, am intrigued.

Kya smiles. "It sounds like you guys are interested! Everyone change into your swimsuits, and meet us down at the beach!"

After everyone has gathered down at the beach, we are handed our snorkeling gear.

"Everyone is going to swim out to where you see the lights coming up from under the water. The lights attract the manta rays favorite meal: plankton. The manta rays come to feast, while we get to enjoy the show."

*This is going to be fun!*

I put on my mask and swim out to the spot Kya told us to go to. We can't see the plankton, but they must be there because one manta ray shows up, then another and another until there are at least a hundred swimming below us in the water.

It is an incredible sight; manta rays majestically flapping their fins, going in all different kinds of directions. One gets close enough for me to run my hand across its smooth back as it passes under me. I am glad that they don't seem bothered by the audience floating above them.

We must have been there a while because my body is starting to get tired. Thankfully, Kya's family asks us to go back ashore.

They tell us that we are welcome to stay on the beach and enjoy the evening, but I am exhausted, so I head back to my room and fall into a deep sleep.

I am woken up by a knock on my door.

"It's time to leave for Athein, Chartreuse!" Kya says, panicked through the door.

*Oh my gosh!*

I slept in!

"Coming!"

I jump out of bed and throw my clothes into my suitcase. I throw my hair into a ponytail and make my way to the front of Kya's house where *everyone* else is waiting. The Royal Family is already in their limo and so are most of the girls. Daphne is the only one still standing outside of her limo, smiling at me, and not the friendly kind. If I didn't know any better, I would say that she stayed out until I got here just so I could see that smile. I glare at her.

I throw my luggage into the limo.

I collapse into my seat, my heartrate finally dropping on the drive to the airport.

As I am grabbing my things out of the trunk, Reed approaches to take them for me.

He looks me up and down and says, "I was afraid we were going to have to take off without you, sleepy head."

"Shut up." I shove my suitcase into his abdomen.

He chuckles as I walk away.

"You guys are going to love it there!" Daphne is already talking up her province.

I groan, grab one of the furthest seats in the back, put on my headphones, and disappear into my book.

# Chapter 4

We land on the tarmac in Athein, once again greeted by the annoying press.

I put my sunglasses on immediately when stepping off the plane because the sun is so brilliant here. There is a light, salty breeze that helps take the edge off the triple digit temperature.

We hop into the waiting limos and make our way to Daphne's home.

We drive up a long, winding road that borders the beach. It doesn't take us long to reach Daphne's house. It is a huge — No. That doesn't even begin to cover it. It is a ginormous, all glass house. I groan at the lack of privacy I am going to have for the next couple of days.

Daphne has us follow her to her main living area.

"Welcome, everyone, to my home! These are my parents." She points to the beautiful gene pool that made her. "Amara is my mother and Elias is my father." They wave to the rest of us. They don't have that same off-putting, better-than-you air that their daughter has. "The bedrooms are on the third floor. Please find the door with your name on it and make yourselves at home. Dinner will be served on the back patio at six. If you get hungry between now and then, there is a marvelous spread of finger food in the kitchen for you to munch on." She looks straight at me with that last sentence. A smug, knowing smile plastered on her stupid, perfect face. I glare back. "See everyone tonight!"

With that, I grab my bag, and make my way to the third floor. I see Prince Zane's room is right next to a door without a name on it. I am going to guess hers.

*Gutsy.*

I roll my eyes and continue down the hall. Like I had suspected, she has me at the very end and right across the hall from Reed's?!

*What the eff?! Shouldn't he be right by Zane's?!*

Before I can get a frustrated groan out, a familiar voice greets me.

"Hello, possible future princess."

I turn to see Reed carrying a bag to his room.

"Hello. Looks like Daphne wants Zane all to herself."

He chuckles. "I am not shocked. She is constantly throwing herself at him. It's really annoying, actually."

It's my turn to chuckle.

"Since I am out of work for the time being, shout out for me if you ever need a bodyguard."

"I can take care of myself, thank you very much." I open my door and enter. As I am about to shut the door, I see Reed staring at me with a crooked smile. I glare back and close the door to him chuckling.

Even though my stomach is eating itself, I refuse to have Daphne catch me at her precious finger food table. I grab a water bottle from the mini fridge in my room and down it, hoping to satisfy my stomach for the time being.

I decide to get myself ready for dinner early and go find Kya. I pick out my black, belted jumpsuit that sits nice and flowy everywhere. I am covered from my ankles to my neck and out past my shoulders, but the lightweight fabric will allow me to stay cool. I throw my hair into a curly ponytail and begin my search for Kya.

I start by knocking on her door. No answer. I wonder where she could be. It shouldn't be too hard since all the outer walls are glass. I go down the stairs and spot her out by the pool, lounging in a chair.

"May I join you?" I ask her.

"Absolutely!" She smiles.

We both take a cleansing breath and lean back in our chairs.

"You ever been to Athein before?" she asks.

"I have. My family and I take a trip down here every year. You?"

"I have been once before, but it was a long time ago. It's a lovely place, isn't it?"

"Very much so."

"Do you miss the snow?"

"Not yet."

We both laugh.

"It's beautiful in its own way." I continue. "But being in the warm and sun is always a nice change though."

We sit in silence for a few minutes.

"Have you been alone with Zane yet?"

"I have. Have you?"

"He asked me to accompany him after dinner for a walk around the property." She blushes furiously.

"Kya! That is awesome!" I am very happy for her.

"It is, isn't it?" She can't stop smiling. I can tell she likes Zane very much.

"Well, you enjoy yourself tonight."

"I am pretty sure I will."

The dinner bell dings to announce it is ready. Everyone congregates on the back patio. I have to hand it to Daphne, it's beautiful. There is a strand of lights crisscrossing above us, lit torches along the railing, and candles illuminating the long table. It is covered in a lacy tablecloth with fine china and spotless silverware on top.

Everyone takes a seat with Daphne and her family on one end, the Royal Family on the other, and the rest of us in between.

They reveal the first course. There are kabobs of various roasted meats, pita bread, fresh tomatoes and cucumbers, and a tzatziki sauce. This is my favorite dish from here.

Everyone prepares their sandwiches. Moans rise from all around the table.

"This is delicious, Mr. and Mrs. Starling," Zane politely says.

"Thank you very much, Your Highness." Mrs. Starling beams at the compliment.

Servants make their way around the table, pouring ouzo for everyone. This is *not* something I am fond of. I am not a fan of black licorice.

I take a small sip so that I am not rude, but also so I don't choke on the bold flavor. My plan doesn't work. A small cough escapes me.

"You ok over there, Chartreuse?" Daphne asks.

She is not asking out of concern, but out of trying to humiliate me.

"Yes, thank you."

"Not a fan of ouzo?"

"I am not." I can feel everyone's eyes on me.

*Kill me now.*

"What are you a fan of?"

"I am drawn to drinks with cranberry in them. I love fruity drinks."

"Have you ever had 'Sex on the Beach'?"

My eyes go wide, and I feel my face turn bright red. A few

utensils crash down onto their plates. She has a smug smile on her face. I say nothing.

"It is a drink with vodka, peach, orange, lime, and cranberry in it," Reed explains.

I turn to him. I never thought I would think this, but thank God for Reed. He has a small, sympathetic smile on his face.

I smile back and nod my head to let him know how grateful I am.

I turn back to Daphne. "I have not, but it sounds like something I would absolutely *love* to try."

Now she's the one to blush while some quiet giggles break out around the table.

She backs down and we all get back to eating.

I am beyond relieved when dessert is rice pudding and not baklava like my family usually gets. I have a hard time being ladylike with that delicious, sticky treat.

Once dinner is done, everyone disperses to different areas on the property. I find a secluded patch of grass, lay myself down, and gaze up at the stars. I think back over all that happened at dinner: Daphne being her usual antagonistic self and Reed *being nice to me*. That is what has got my head really reeling. Not that I am not grateful, just confused. We don't like each other. I decide to not read into it too much and enjoy the blanket of stars above me.

# Chapter 5

Daphne let us know at breakfast that we would be on the beach until our departure for Estar later in the day.

I put on my black, high-waisted two piece with a haltered, ruffle top. I complete the look with my flip flops and a sun hat, and make my way down to the beach.

It is dreadfully apparent that my skin tone is much brighter than the rest of the beach goers. I am going to blind someone. I find an empty umbrella and park myself under it.

Daphne and Kya have found spots along the beach to catch some sun while Jazzie is in a beach chair surfing her phone. Zane chooses her as his next alone time target. They take off, walking along the edge of the beach.

Someone clears their throat behind me. "Is this spot taken?"

I turn to see Reed. I shake my head and scoot to give him some room.

"Thank you." He gives me a smile.

"You're welcome." I return with a *small* smile.

"Not a tanning girl, huh?"

"I have only two shades: snow white and lobster red. I don't feel like having to treat a sunburn on this trip."

"I don't blame you. I am the same way."

I look at him. It makes sense with that fiery red hair of his. It looks good against the backdrop of the sandy beach.

*What the eff?!*

I quickly return my gaze to the ocean before he notices me staring at his hair.

We sit in silence for a few minutes.

"Come on. We can't waste a perfectly good beach day," he says.

I turn to look at him. "Even if you would be able to get me out from under this umbrella, which you won't, I didn't bring any sunscreen."

He pulls out a bottle, spins it in the air, and catches it.

I narrow my eyes at him.

"Come on."

I sigh. "Fine."

He gives me the bottle, I squirt some into my hands, and get to work covering myself up. I notice him moving a lot, so I glance at him.

*Dear heavens.*

He is shirtless. My eyes go big. His chiseled chest and six pack are sprinkled with freckles. His arms are incredibly defined as well.

*Why is it getting hard to breathe?*

He catches me. I quickly get back to the sunscreen. I finish covering myself, except for my back, and hand the bottle over to him without looking at him. I am positive he thinks I am being weird.

He breaks the silence a couple of minutes later. "Here, let me get your back."

I go stiff and my heart starts racing. "I already got it."

"No, you didn't. I was right here."

*Dangit.*

"Please?"

I sigh. "Ok." I turn my back to him.

I expect him to place it directly onto my back and have that horrible cold sensation. However, he must have rubbed it in his hands first because it is nice and warm. My breath catches. The whole time his hands are gliding across my back, I can only take shallow breaths.

"There. Do me?"

I grab the bottle and he turns around. My word, his back is just as fit as the rest of him. I do him the same courtesy and rub the lotion in my hands before applying it to him.

I take a breath before placing my hands on his back. I start at the top, across his broad shoulders. Then move downward and my hands start to tremble when they land in that dip along his spine.

I remove my hands and clear my throat. "Done."

"Thank you."

"You're welcome and thank you."

"No problem. Now, shall we?" He stands and offers me his hand.

I raise an eyebrow, then grab it.

We make our way to the water's edge. My feet hit the water. I stop and let the waves roll over my feet, slowly covering them in sand. I close my eyes and soak up the sun. This feeling never gets old; feeling the sun slowly penetrate each layer of skin until you almost feel its heat in your bones.

I feel a splash of cold water on me. I gasp and open my eyes to see Reed smiling mischievously at me.

"What the heck?!"

"You have to get more than your feet wet." He bends over, getting ready to splash more water on me.

"No, you don't!" I gather up a handful of water and launch it at him first. It gets him right in the face.

*Yes!*

He looks back at me.

*Uh oh.*

He gives me that same smile when he first splashed me. I take off running down the beach, water splashing up as I go. I can hear him following close behind. I don't dare turn around.

It doesn't take long until he grabs me around the waist, stopping me. He swoops me out and makes his way further out into the ocean.

I start kicking and wiggling. "No! Reed, don't!"

He flings me into the water.

I emerge, now giving him the mischievous look. I sweep my hands across the water, sending waves at him. He reciprocates.

After a few minutes, we tire and stand there laughing.

I look at him. He looks good wet; with his hair flattened against his head and water dripping down that sculpted body of his.

*Snap out of it!*

We head back onto the beach.

"Thank you, Reed. I had fun." I smile.

He nods. "You're welcome."

We get back under the safety of the umbrella for the rest of the day until it's time to take off for Estar.

✦

Estar is hot and dry. The only moisture on me here is my own sweat.

As we are driving to Jazzie's home, I look out the window and see an interesting sight. There are thin clouds stretching down from the mass of clouds above it, like I've seen when it rains. The weird thing about what I am seeing is, the clouds do not reach the ground. Jazzie must have read my mind.

"It's so hot here, that sometimes the rain evaporates before it hits the ground."

I look at her. "Wow." I look back out the window.

"Yeah, *wow*," she says, sarcastically.

We pull up to a geometric house. It was a perfect square, with a flat roof and brilliant sharp corners. The walls were glass with clay borders for the edges.

"Your house is beautiful, Jazzie."

"Thank you."

*Whoa, did she just say that?*

After we have come to a stop and have all gathered outside, we exchange confused glances between each other. King Harden looks to Jazzie and asks, "Where are your parents?"

"They are out amongst the people. They do it quite often, especially with this rough year."

He nods to her and says, "Lead the way."

We all file behind Jazzie as she leads us around and past her house, out of a metal gate. There is a trail that we walk down that takes us over a small hill. Once we reach the crest, we see the rest of the city. It is filled with similar houses made of clay and flat roofs. There is a large street filled with colorful tents lining the edges for what had to be a mile. Jazzie takes us down to this street.

Unlike the lively market that Zane and I perused back in Loshia, this one is filled with solemn, quiet faces.

As our group starts walking down the street, whispers and sideways looks start rising up from the people. I have a feeling I know why, after what Jazzie told me. My feeling is confirmed as we pass by mostly empty tents. Their usual crop yields are almost zero here. My heart hurts for them.

Our group abruptly stops. I peek around to the front where Jazzie, King Harden, Queen Gabrielle, and Zane are. There is a small group of people blocking the road, looking very angry.

"What is the meaning of this?" King Harden demands.

"Why has our king and queen ignored our pleas for help?"

"We have not ignored them. We have had meetings and concluded that we would determine the aid after our visit here."

The man who asked the question, steps closer to the King. He doesn't move, but everyone else moves back.

"While you were having your *meetings*, we have been struggling!"

"I am sorry for that, but we are here now, and will determine the aid after we have assessed the need."

The man reaches behind him and one of the guards yells, "Knife!" In a flash, guards have surrounded the Royal Family and have them running back out of the city. This, of course, has the rest of us about-facing and running too. We can hear the angry crowd behind us yelling. I turn my head and see them pursuing us.

We run up and over the hill and into Jazzie's gates. The guards slam them shut and point their guns at the crowd that has caught up outside. They are throwing their fists into the air and shouting obscenities.

"Come." Jazzie commands, and we all follow inside her house.

After we have all gathered inside, King Harden looks at Jazzie. "What was that?! Why didn't you stop your people?!"

Jazzie looks unfazed. "I sympathize with my people. I was letting them be heard."

"They tried to assassinate me!"

"I had no idea they had a knife! They wouldn't have been successful, your guards had you plenty protected."

"I don't care! This is unacceptable! You will face punishment! Where are your parents?!"

Queen Gabrielle has grabbed her husband's arm. "Calm down! Let's wait for her parents and have a civil talk about this."

King Harden looks down at his wife. "I will wait for her parents, but I am not promising anything about the repercussions." He glares back at Jazzie, and walks out of the room.

Jazzie, who has only ever shown indifference, looks nervous. It's unsettling.

I see Zane walk over to Reed and ask, "What should we do?"

Reed folds his arms across his chest.

"Well, *something* has to be done. These kinds of action against the crown cannot happen."

I start taking slow steps toward them, still listening.

"Like what?"

"I am not going to lie, this is pretty serious Zane. I believe that someone has to be made an example of. I say the one that drew the knife."

I start walking faster. "Excuse me?"

They both turn to look at me.

"Miss Moore? Sorry, Chartreuse?" Zane greets.

"Can I add my opinion to this discussion?" I ask.

I see Reed narrow his eyes at me. I don't pay him any attention.

"Absolutely."

"Thank you, Zane. Even though what happened was scary and wrong, I don't think violence is the way to go."

Reed scoffs. "Oh really? And how would *you* address the situation?"

"Think about it. These people are suffering, and for a long time it seems. They are tired, hungry, frustrated, and angry. I say that you hear them out and help them. Show mercy."

"No," Reed snaps.

Zane and I both look at him.

"You cannot let something like this go unpunished. If you do, whenever anyone else has a grievance with the crown, they will think they can answer in a like manner."

"Forgive me, *Reed*, but this is a pretty big grievance. Their Crown hasn't helped them in a great time of need."

"They were going to." Reed is now facing me and not Zane.

"After a long time of not doing so." My voice is raising.

"Be careful, Miss Moore, you are murmuring against the crown."

"Is that a threat?"

"If you don't back down."

I was about to keep going when Zane interrupts, "Enough! Both of you. You have both given me something to think about and share with my father. I need time to think, please leave me."

Reed and I both look at Zane then back at each other. I stomp past Reed and out the back doors.

The jerk must have followed me.

"You have no idea how any of this works; protecting the Royal Family." Reed says from behind me.

I spin around. "And you have no idea what compassion is like, or when it is needed. These people *need* it." I turn back around and keep walking.

"Compassion is weakness."

I stop in front of Jazzie's stables and turn to face him. "Sometimes, compassion is strength."

I am staring straight into his eyes as he approaches. They are glaring back at me, intensely.

"You are so ignorant. I hope he doesn't listen to you."

"*Excuse me*?! You are —"

I see Reed's face turn to stone as he looks past me. I turn to see what he is looking at.

All the people at the gate are gone, and for good reason. There is a wall of sand barreling towards us.

My eyes go big. I turn to look back at the house.

"There's no time." Reed grabs my hand and pulls me towards the entrance of the stables. Sand starts to hit our faces. We cover them as we make it to the doors and shut them. Reed runs to the other side and shuts those doors as well. He sighs and leans back against the wall.

"Don't think you're getting a thank you." I snap at him.

"I wasn't expecting one." He looks towards me. "Although, that is quite ungrateful of you."

I roll my eyes and turn around. "I am pretty sure your ego can handle it."

He scoffs behind me. "My ego? What about yours?!" He sounds close.

I turn around to find him right behind me. Surprised, I take a step back.

He tilts his head to the side. "What?" He takes a small step towards me.

"Am I making you nervous?" He takes another one.

I scoff. "Not at all. And by the way, there is that ego again." I take another step back and run into the wall.

*Shoot.*

He takes another step and is right in front of me, staring down at me. I stare back.

My heart is beating out of my chest. Not from fear, like the arrogant jerk thought, but something else. Excitement?

*What the eff?*

He puts his arms on the wall, boxing me in. My heart goes even crazier.

"You infuriate me." He says.

I narrow my eyes. "The feeling is mutual."

He smirks. Why was it so sexy? My breath catches.

A bang against the barn pulls us out of our little battle. We both back away from the wall.

"How long do sandstorms last?" I ask.

"However long or short they want to be."

"Thanks. That was so helpful."

I walk away and find myself a bale of hay.

I lean my head back and close my eyes. Reed sounds like he does something similar.

We sit there and listen to the howling wind outside, causing things to bang against the barn off and on.

My mind starts to wander, thinking about how different our

Estar visit could have been. I think about how we have missed out on touring Jazzie's province, getting to see the various crops. I think about much I wanted to ride a camel. I think about Daphne and a camel … I chuckle out loud.

"What?" Reed asks.

"Oh, I was just thinking how a camel encounter with Daphne would have gone."

"How would it have gone?"

"I see her cautiously approaching it. I see her putting her hand on it and —"

"It sneezes on her?"

I chuckle again. "Yep."

Reed chuckles too. "That would have been awesome to see."

I lean my head up and open my eyes. Reed is still leaning back with his eyes closed, a faint smile on his lips. He has his hand clasped across his stomach and his legs are outstretched and crossed. I smile to myself and return to my previous position.

⁂

Except for the occasional neigh from a horse, silence fills the stables. It seems the storm has passed.

Reed and I head out the doors to find everything covered in a light layer of sand. We make our way into Jazzie's house.

Everyone is gathered in a semi-circle around King Harden, Queen Gabrielle, Zane, Jazzie, and who I would presume are her parents. Reed and I plant ourselves around the outside, near the front.

"The actions from earlier today, were inexcusable. Lives could have been lost." King Harden announced.

Jazzie and her parents' faces are neutral, I can't tell what they are feeling. I, however, am getting nervous.

"Because of that, Jazzie will no longer be allowed to vie for Prince Zane's hand."

Whispers rumble through the room. I am relieved to hear that that is all he demanding as retribution. I wonder if my words with Zane helped with that.

"I have also heard Estar's pleas, more so after earlier. The crown promises to send monetary assistance along with manpower to help recover the crops. We will also ask the whole kingdom to join us in prayer, that water will soon fall upon this province."

Jazzie and her parents nod in approval.

I am ecstatic to hear about the assistance the royal family will be giving to Jazzie's people. Not thinking, I grasp Reed's arm. I look up at him, after realizing what I had done. He looks down at me and raises an eyebrow. I withdraw my hands quickly, embarrassed. I see one of those sexy smirks again as he looks back front. I can't help but feel my face getting warm.

*Awkward.*

"Because of the decision to remove Jazzie from courting Prince Zane, and having taken care of arrangements for Estar's aid, we have no reason to stay here any longer. We will be heading for Aspil tonight. Miss Moore? I suggest you give your family a heads up."

I nod and make my way to an empty hallway to make the call.

"Hello?" My sister asks.

"Hey. Can you get dad on the phone?"

"Hey! We are so excited for you guys to be coming here tomorrow!"

"Yeah, me too. Things have changed a little bit. Get dad for me please?"

"Why can't you tell me?"

"I would rather tell dad."

"He's busy."

No he wasn't. Her curiosity is just too piqued to hand over the phone.

I sigh. "We are heading over tonight." I pull the phone away from my ear.

"What?!"

I could still hear her.

"Yep, but we will be getting there pretty late so all you guys have to worry about is making sure lodging is set up, ok?"

"Yeah! No problem! I can't believe Prince Zane will be in our house!"

"Yep, it's pretty awesome." I say with sarcasm thinking about all the ways my sister could embarrass me while everyone is there. "Hey, I gotta go, we're taking off."

"Ok! Love you! See you soon!"

Before I can even reply, she hangs up.

Everyone is heading out to the waiting limos. I have to talk to Jazzie before I leave.

"Hey. I am really sorry about you not being able to join us."

"It's ok. Zane isn't really my type."

"Too nice?"

*Ouch. Too soon?*

She grins. "A little."

*Whew.*

"I am glad that your people are finally getting the help that they need."

"Me too."

We both stare at the floor in awkward silence for a minute. I look up and see that everyone else is already in their limos.

"Well, I'd better go. Keep in touch?"

"Maybe."

We smile at each other, then I make my way to the driveway, and get into my limo, alone.

# Chapter 6

I am nervous as we drive to my house from the airport. Not because we are once again surrounded on all sides by reporters, but because I can picture my parents standing there, polite and regal, and my sister bouncing up and down like she has to pee.

*Please Violet.*

When we pull up to my house, I am relieved to see her standing just as still as my parents. I let out a breath, open my door, and cannot keep the smile off my face as my family and I meet eyes.

I hug my dad first.

"How are you doing, sweet pea?"

"I am doing great. Happy to be home for a little bit."

I move to my mom.

"So happy to have you home!"

"I haven't even been gone for a week." I give her a side smile.

"I know, but it's the longest you've been gone."

"I know."

Lastly, I hug my sister.

"No jumping or squealing? Did you get bad news while I was gone? Are you dying?"

"Hey! I can be a proper lady."

I raise my eyebrow at her and smile. "Yes, you can. I am proud of you."

Somehow, she straightens up even more.

I turn to all my guests, introduce my family, and let everyone head to their rooms.

I sit with my family in the living room and catch them up on everything from the past few days. Violet was her typical self whenever anything romantic was mentioned.

"So, are you and this Reed, like friends?!" My sister asks.

"What part of anything that I have told you about him implies *friendship*?!"

"He was excited to have you sit next to him, you had a fun time together at the beach, and, I don't know, he saved your life?!"

*Hm.*

"No. We are just being able to tolerate each other now."

My mom and sister look at each other and say, "Mm hm." My dad is just looking at me with his head in his hand, as if he's thinking.

"Oh, you can't be thinking the same thing as them?!" I don't even give him a chance to answer. "You know what, I am tired and going to bed." I give them all a kiss. "Goodnight!"

I collapse onto my bed. It feels so good to be on it again. The beds in the palace are wonderful and all, but nothing beats the familiarity and comfort that *my* bed brings.

Despite being back in my own bed, I have a hard time falling asleep. I can't get the conversation with my family out of my head. Reed and I are *not* friends ... Are we?

⚜

When everyone is gathered around our table for breakfast, my parents announce that we are going to be ice skating.

*Yes!*

I am so glad that they chose something I can do well in front of everyone. They wanted the activity to be a surprise for me as well, so they didn't tell me last night.

I run up to my room, layer up, and make my way to the pond. I want to get some alone time on the ice before everyone else shows up.

I lace up my skates, step out onto the ice, and push off. I close my eyes and take in my surroundings; the brisk air on my face and the sound of my skates slicing through the thick ice.

I am able to make a full lap around the pond and land a jump before others begin to join me. Kya is the first. You can tell she has had experience on the ice. Even though she can't do any tricks, she makes her way gracefully around.

Zane and Reed are next. They seem to be along the lines of Kya. Zane approaches her and they enjoy taking laps together, while Reed hangs back giving them space.

Daphne is one of the last to show, followed closely by my family. My parents and sister join the rest of us, while Daphne wobbles her way to the edge. She steps onto the ice carefully with her first foot. When the other one joins it, wham! She falls to the ice.

I hold back a laugh. If she were anyone else, I would feel bad for her, but this is Daphne. She has embarrassed me and made me feel inferior. This is justice.

Should I help?

*No.*

I should probably help her.

*Probably.*

I sigh and make my way over to her.

She is on all fours, trying unsuccessfully to get up. She reminds me of a newborn foal. I hold out my hand. She bats it away.

"Really?" I ask irritated.

"I don't need your help."

"That's not what it looks like from up here, and it probably looks the same to everyone else too." I gesture my hands to the small group of people out here with us.

She looks at them, then me, and grabs my hand. I pull her to her feet. I let her go the second she has her feet beneath her and take off.

"That was kind of you." An all too familiar voice says coming up beside me.

"Eh. It was the right thing to do."

"I am a bad person then, because I would have let her struggle."

I look at Reed and see him smiling to himself. I can't help smiling too.

"Believe me, it crossed my mind."

"I am sure."

"What's that supposed to mean?!"

"We seem to be cut from the same cloth, Miss Moore, or can I say Chartreuse?"

It is weird hearing him say my first name. I kind of like it, it sounds nice.

"You can call me Chartreuse, but how in the world are we cut from the same cloth?"

"We are both stubborn and ornery. I am assuming you had to hold back a laugh?"

I look away from him. "No …"

"See?"

"Oh, shut up, Reed."

I pick up my pace, leaving him behind, chuckling to himself. *Jerk.*

The thing is? The jerk isn't wrong.

As all our guests are in various places around the house, warming up, I am helping my folks set up our heated solarium for dinner.

It's supposed to be a clear night, so our goal is to not detract from the natural beauty of the night sky. We add strings of white lights around the border of the room. We place several white, three-wick candles down the center of the glass table. Fresh, evergreen branches swerve in and out between all the candles. Sparkling crystal, white porcelain, and spotless silverware are placed in front of each seat.

"Why don't you go on ahead and get dressed for dinner, dear. We can finish up here," my mother says, smiling.

"Are you sure?"

"Yes."

I hand the rest of the place cards to my mother and head up to my room.

I start to browse through my evening gowns in my closet, but it doesn't take long for me to decide on what to wear.

I choose a blue to white, ombre sleeveless dress. The bodice is covered in rhinestones that slowly space themselves further out as you go down the dress. It has sheer sleeves with sporadic rhinestones on it as well. A sheer, floor-length cape drapes out from my shoulders.

I put my hair up into an elegant, braided bun. I add sparkles to it. I finish with dangling diamond earrings that almost hit my shoulders.

I look in the mirror. Other than wishing I had piercing blue eyes to make the outfit come fully together, I like what I see.

I make my way downstairs and position myself, along with my family, at the entrance to the solarium.

Kya is the first to show, followed by Daphne who greets me warmly.

*Faker.*

Next, is the Royal Family, with Zane stopping in front of me, taking my hand, and planting a tender kiss on the back of it.

"You look lovely this evening, Chartreuse."

"Thank you, Zane." I smile warmly.

I turn and look at Reed who is bringing up the rear. He is just standing there, staring at me, with an expression that I can't read.

I raise an eyebrow. He shakes his head and makes his way down the greeting line.

When he gets to me, he gives a bow. I curtsy.

"You, um ..." He clears his throat. "You look very nice."

"You don't need to compliment me just because you are in front of my parents." I whisper.

"I mean it. Even if your parents weren't here, I would still tell you the same thing."

I look into his eyes, which seem softened. "Thank you."

He gives me another bow before heading into the room with the others.

I let out a breath that I didn't realize I'd been holding. I feel eyes on me and turn to see my whole family staring me with smirks.

I roll my eyes. "It's not like that."

Their smirks grow wider.

I groan. "Let's eat. Please." I go and find my seat.

Hot mulled wine is poured into everyone's glasses. It is a flavorful drink that makes you feel warm inside and out.

We start with a comforting cabbage soup, followed by elk with oven fried potatoes and carrots.

"This meal is hardy and delicious Mr. and Mrs. Moore," Zane says.

"Thank you very much, Your Highness," my mother replies.

"I killed and processed the elk myself," my father shares proudly.

"Well done. I may need to take you hunting with me sometime," King Harden says, smiling.

"I would love to join you, Your Majesty."

Everyone continues eating.

"I can see where Chartreuse gets her beauty, Mrs. Moore."
Daphne pipes in.

I look at her and narrow my eyes.

My mother is giggling beside me. "Well, thank you, dear."

Daphne's gaze meets mine and gives me a smirk.

*That little …*

My sister kicks my leg under the table.

"Ow!" I say quietly, glaring at her.

She nods down the table.

I turn and see Reed quickly look back down to his plate.

I lean over to Violet. "What?"

"That guy can't keep his eyes off of you."

I look at Reed again, who is still focused on his dinner, then
back at her. "There is no way."

"There is. And look! He's doing it again."

I sneakily look out of the corner of my eye. Sure enough, he's
looking right at me.

My breath catches again.

*Stop it.*

Dessert is brought out, a decadent, chocolate, molten lava
cake.

I take it as a hit, based on all the satisfactory moans that rise
up around the room. I grin to myself. I am pleased that the visit
to my home has gone so well.

After dinner, everyone disperses into different rooms. All the
women go to the library and all the men congregate in the living
room. I would feel awkward being the only girl with the men and
I really don't feel like being in the same room as Daphne, so I put
on my coat, and head out onto our balcony.

I close my eyes and take in a deep, crisp breath. I open my eyes
and watch my breath coat the city lights below me. Even though I
quite enjoy the temperate weather of Uspon, I have missed this air.

"I have to say, Aspil is my favorite place that we have visited on this trip."

I whirl around and see Reed leaning back against the wall.

"You scared me! When did you get out here?"

"Just a moment ago." He pushes off the wall and joins me at the railing.

I think back to what he just said. "Really?"

"Really what?"

"Aspil is your favorite?"

"It is. Until this trip, I had never been outside of Uspon. I quite enjoy this contrast of climate."

"A lot of people don't like it, but I love it. The air is so refreshing here compared to the other places, especially the more humid ones."

"Agreed. The sky is so clear and bright here."

"It's probably because we are much closer to it." I look back up at the clear, night sky. Countless stars dot it.

"Makes sense."

We stand in silence for a couple of minutes.

"Your family is really nice."

I smile. "Yeah, they're pretty great."

He chuckles softly.

"It makes me wonder where you came from."

"Hey!" I smack his arm.

We both laugh.

"Are you looking forward to being back in Uspon tomorrow?" He asks.

"What is it with you tonight? Compliments and small talk?" I give him a side glance. "Are you sick?"

He smiles. "Maybe I am just warming up to you."

"That's ironic considering where we are at." I smile back.

He studies my face. I see his eyes focus on my lips. My heart skips. He looks back to my eyes.

"Goodnight Chartreuse."

"Goodnight."

He turns and goes inside.

Even though it is in the single digits, I don't feel cold. I am surprisingly warm all over; and it's not from the alcohol.

# Chapter 7

The next morning, we all pack our things, and make our way to the limos that will take us to the airport and back to Uspon.

I kiss my mom and sister goodbye then give my dad a hug. As we are holding each other, he whispers, "You have caught the eye of more than one man."

I pull back and look into his eyes, knowing what he meant.

*That was made apparent yesterday.*

I give him a small smile and a slight nod. I find my limo and take a seat. As the line of cars pull out, I wave out the window to my family.

The whole flight to Uspon, I think back on the last week and all my interactions with Reed. They have been full of everything but niceness — until last night. *Things have changed a little bit, haven't they?*

I smile to myself, knowing that I get to spend a little more time at Uspon … And Reed.

Ms. Maren greets all of us ladies on the castle's front steps.

"The Royal Family has matters to attend to for the next couple of days, so you will all get to enjoy a couple days of downtime."

I smile. This is just what I need after spending nearly a week meeting lots of new people and needing to be proper.

I make my way up to my room and collapse onto my bed.

"Did you have a good trip, miss?" Elise asks upon entering my room.

"I did." I smile. "How did you do while I was gone?"

She smiles back. "I did just fine, thank you. Do you need me to help you unpack?"

"No, thank you. I will be fine. Could you please let me know when lunch is ready, though?"

"Absolutely, miss." She gives a small bow and exits my room.

I get up and start to unpack my things. When I walk by my window, I see that the royal family is outside having tea. Reed is not far from the group, standing at attention.

He is quite a handsome man. I think back to all our nice moments with each other. I smile. I also think back to all of our more *ornery* moments with each other. I chuckle. As if he could sense my presence, he turns his head to my window. I quickly hide behind my wall.

*Crap! Did he see me?*

I dare a peek out the window. He is back to facing forward, but there is a small grin on his face.

*Crap. He did.*

Elise lets me know that lunch is ready a couple of hours later. I join the other ladies in the dining room. We are served egg salad sandwiches with iced tea.

Daphne clears her throat. "I have been invited by Zane to spend the afternoon with him," she says proudly.

Kya and I stare at her. "Cool." I say. "That's kind of why we're here."

She scoffs. "Have you guys spent time *alone* with Zane?"

We both nod. "Even Jazzie had a turn before she was eliminated," Kya says.

"Hmph. He must have saved the best for last." She smiles to herself.

I roll my eyes and we all go back to eating.

I can't eat fast enough. I want to get out of here before Daphne gets picked up for her date with Zane. Alas, I am too slow. Her sickening, "Of course I will join Prince Zane!" to the servant that is escorting her, almost makes me lose my lunch.

I excuse myself from the table and make my way to the library.

I inhale deeply, taking in the scent of the various types of paper that made up the books. I walk around, running my fingers along the spines of the books on the ground floor, each one making my fingers tingle. The knowledge or adventures that lie within the pages makes me giddy.

I grab a couple of books from the first floor then ascend to the second and third, grabbing a few more. I have a nice stack cradled in my arms when I decide to head back to my room to crack into them. I take one last look around the library before heading out when I run into someone.

"Oof! I am so sorry —" I see his piercing brown eyes. "Reed."

He chuckles and picks up the books I have dropped, returning them to my arms.

"That is quite an armful you have there."

"I may have gotten a little carried away." I smile.

"May I help?"

"Sure." I hand over half the pile.

We make our way to my room. He opens the door for me and follows me in. I lead him to my bookshelf, where we unload the books.

After I get the books the way I want them, I turn and see Reed looking nervously at me with his hands in his pockets.

"Well, this is my room." I say, motioning to my room.

"I see that."

"Yep."

We stand in awkward silence.

"Wait. Aren't you supposed to be with Zane on his date with Daphne?"

"I was, but I couldn't stand being around her anymore. All her overdone sweetness and bragging started to drive me nuts. Zane could see that and dismissed me. He'll be fine."

"I'm sure he will."

Another awkward pause.

"Would you like to come with me and steal some pastries from the kitchen?" He asks, excitedly.

I can't hide my smile. "That sounds great."

When we reach the kitchen, he tells me to wait outside the door. I watch him slide in, grab a couple of flaky treats off a silver tray, and make his way back to me without being noticed.

"Nice!" I say, grabbing one of the sweets.

"Follow me."

He leads us out a servant side door and to a bench. He motions for me to sit down beside him. I happily oblige.

I take a small, lady-like bite out of my pastry.

He grunts. "We both know you want to dig into that thing. No need to eat like a lady in front of me."

I think for a moment, then take a big bite. I see him do the same. My mouth is filled with the delicate bread and a sweet almond paste.

"Mm. Thank you."

"You're welcome."

We chew for a moment.

"Do you do this often? Sneak treats from the kitchen?"

"Very."

I chuckle. "You are more than welcome to invite me again anytime."

He looks at me, smiling. "Will do."

The silence that follows isn't awkward as we finish up our pastries.

"So, how long have you been Zane's bodyguard?"

"Since I was old enough to join the Royal Guard when I was sixteen, so five years."

"Is that when you guys became friends, too?"

"No, we have been friends much longer than that."

"Is he the reason why you joined the Royal Guard?"

"I was *hoping* to become his personal guard, but even if I hadn't, I would've still wanted to join. It's something I have always wanted to do."

"What made you want to join?"

"You are full of questions today." He raises a brow at me. "My turn."

"Sorry. Go ahead."

"Have you always loved to read?"

"I have."

"Do you have a favorite book?"

"I don't, there are too many. I could *possibly* tell you a favorite out of each genre?" I think for a moment. "Nope, I can't even do that."

He laughs. It sends chills up and down my spine, the good kind.

We hear voices approaching, Zane and Daphne's.

"Hide!" Reed grabs my hand and pulls me behind a massive shrub. We sit completely still as their voices come and go. Reed still has a hold of my hand.

I look down at our joined hands, then up at him. He looks down, blushes furiously, and let's go.

"Sorry."

"It's ok." I can feel heat rising to my cheeks too.

He rubs the back of his head.

"I should probably check on Zane."

*Darn.*

"Yeah, probably."

We both get up and enter the castle again through the side door.

"Thanks again, Reed."

"You're welcome." He stares at me. "See you around, Chartreuse."

"See you."

We separate and go in different directions. I wipe my sweaty, shaky hands on my clothes as I make my way back to my room. I hope I don't run into anyone because I do *not* want to have to explain the huge smile that's plastered on my face.

# Chapter 8

I knew the Royal Family was going to be busy again today, but I still hoped that I would run into Reed sometime, just like we did yesterday. I didn't.

I wasn't in the mood to socialize with the other ladies, so I take my dinner in my room. I look out my window and notice while I eat, that it's a clear night. So when I finish eating, I go outside to the gardens.

I find a nice, secluded spot, lay down on the grass, and face the sparkling sky. A clear night always brings me peace. It doesn't matter if it's in my cold Aspil or temperate Uspon, the stars make me happy.

"May I join you?"

My heart skips a beat. I look over and see Reed. "Please."

He lays down next to me. "Beautiful night."

"It is." I take a few breaths before asking, "Busy day?"

"It was." He pauses. "Don't tell me you missed me?"

My face feels hot. "No. I am just not used to *not* seeing you." *Smooth.*

I hear him chuckle next to me. "You missed me."

I turn my head to him. "I think *you* missed *me*! Who had to find me tonight?"

He turns to me and searches my face, but doesn't say anything.

*Ha.*

We look back at the stars.

"Do you have a favorite constellation?" I ask.

"It would have to be the Little Dipper."

"How come?"

"Because it contains the North Star. I like having a constant compass at night."

"Very nice."

"What about you?"

Without hesitation, I answer, "Andromeda."

"Don't even have to think about it, huh?"

"Nope. I am sucker for heroes rescuing the damsels in distress."

"Women."

"Hey!" I am looking at him now. "Like you haven't pictured yourself being the hero?"

He turns to face me. "No one has ever needed me to rescue them. Even if they did, I don't really fit the hero description."

I furrow my brows. "What do you mean?"

"I am not rich or powerful." He nods towards the castle. "Or a prince. I am just a lowly commoner who watches the hero get the girl."

My heart starts beating faster. "Titles and power don't matter. You will be a hero in someone's story."

His eyes stare into mine, making my breath hitch. "Do titles and power not mean anything to you?"

"Not at all."

"Then why are you here?"

I pause before answering. "I didn't have anyone pursuing me back home, and what girl wouldn't jump at the chance to be wooed by a prince?"

"Are you happy you came?"

I search his face. "I am."

"Even if you don't end up with Zane?"

I look deep into his eyes and answer truthfully. "Yes."

Something in his eyes change. His eyes go from mine to my lips and back up again. All oxygen escapes me. He starts to roll towards me. My ribs feel like they are about to shatter from my pounding heart. His hand cups my face, he leans closer, and our lips connect.

Warmth bursts out from my lips and spreads throughout my entire body. He lingers there for just a moment before pulling away, keeping his hand on my face. He looks at me and strokes my cheek.

"Good," he says.

# Chapter 9

I sit at the table the next morning, drawing circles in my oatmeal as I think back to last night. Reed *kissed* me! I smile. My thoughts are interrupted when Ms. Maren comes in.

"Good morning, ladies."

"Good morning, Ms. Maren," we answer in unison.

"Prince Zane would like to have a private outing with all of you ladies today."

A gasp from Daphne, a giggle from Kya, and a smile from me, show Ms. Maren how we feel about it.

"You will be going on a hike and picnic with His Highness. So, I suggest you dress appropriately for the occasion."

Daphne is the first to get up and run from the room. Kya and I exit together.

"This is so exciting! It has been a few days since we have gotten him to ourselves."

"Yes, it has." I smile.

I am pretty sure that, even though I am still excited for today, that I am not *as* excited as Kya and Daphne. At least, not in the same way. I am more looking forward to seeing Reed join us.

I go up to my room. Elise is there, waiting to help me get ready.

"I'll be good, Elise. You go ahead and do whatever else needs to be done."

"Are you sure, miss?"

I smile. "I am. I'll see you later."

She bows and exits.

I put on a pair of jean shorts, black tank top, and my black tennis shoes. Part of me wishes that I had hiking boots, but I hate how they accentuate my already large feet with how clunky they are.

I throw my hair back into a ponytail and cover all my exposed skin with sunscreen. I really don't want to end up looking like a beet after today.

I grab my water bottle and head downstairs.

Zane is already waiting at the entrance, with Reed behind him.

"Hello, Chartreuse." Zane smiles.

"Hello, Zane." I smile back and move my eyes to Reed, so he gets my smile too.

He returns it.

Kya is next to join us, then Daphne. I don't think the girl has ever gone on a hike in her life. She has left her hair down and wears a silk top with white shorts. Her shoes are simple slip-ons without arch support. I don't even see a water bottle.

Zane clears his throat. "Daphne? Would you like me to run and grab you a water bottle?"

She turns red. "Oh! That would be a good idea, wouldn't it? May I accompany you?"

"Absolutely." He holds out his arm, and she takes it. They leave.

Reed and I share a glance with raised brows. We both look away smiling.

"Shall we?" Zane asks, when they return. He leads the way out.

We cross the gardens and out through the gate. We start crossing the field of grass.

Zane falls in step with Kya. "How are you doing today?"

"I am doing wonderfully. How are you?"

They carry on their conversation as I take in the beautiful day.

The sun is unimpeded from clouds and casts its bright warmth on us. There is a slight breeze to help us keep cool. The grass is a vibrant green with the occasional dandelion dotting it. Reed's red hair looks glorious against it. It is taking a lot of self-restraint to not walk to where he is and enjoy a conversation with him.

"And how are you doing, Chartreuse?" Zane asks.

I smile. "I am doing good. Are you enjoying the hike so far?"

"I am." He smiles back. "Fresh air is good for the body and the soul."

"Yes, it is."

"Are you a fan of hiking?"

"I am. I'm just used to doing it in zero degrees and snowshoes."

He chuckles. "That is quite different, isn't it?"

"For sure."

"Well." He looks behind us. "I should also check on Daphne. Keep enjoying yourself, Chartreuse."

"Thank you. You too."

⚜

Reaching the trees is a welcome relief from the sun baking our skins. There is a slim trail, wide enough for one person at a time, that winds through the variety of deciduous trees. For a little while, it's pretty level and the hike goes comfortably. However, the trail turns into steep inclines. My legs start to burn.

"Shall we take a break, ladies?" Zane asks from up ahead.

"Yes, please," we almost say in unison.

We gladly pull off to a large, fallen tree and sit down. Zane sits down next to me.

"How are you holding up?"

"I'm doing just fine."

"Good, because we still have a little ways to go."

"I am ready for it." I smile.

"Good."

I take a swig from my water. I see Daphne with her shoes off, rubbing her feet. I feel a little bad for her.

Her eyes meet mine. "What're you looking at?" She snips.

I look away. "Nothing."

*Nevermind.*

After a couple more minutes, we take off again. We hike for another hour on inclines, and I feel like my legs are going to fall off. Thankfully, we reach the top of the hill and set up our lunch, meat and cheese sandwiches with chips.

When we're finished, we start the trek down.

It gets very steep quickly. I am having to use a lot of effort, so I don't slide down.

*So much for my legs catching a break.*

Then, it all happens so fast. I hear Daphne lose her footing from behind me and come sliding down, taking out Kya then me. The men hear the commotion and jump out of the way. We quickly go sliding past.

Daphne sounds like a dying bird until we finally make it to a stop. I wiggle my different appendages to assess the damage. Thankfully, nothing seems broken. I see a hand appear in front of me. I take it and see Reed as he helps me to my feet.

"Thank you."

"You're welcome." He does a quick scan of my body.

Zane comes from behind me. Reed lets go of my hand.

"My heavens, Chartreuse, are you alright?" He asks, as he places his hands on my arms and looks me over.

"Just some scrapes, I'll be fine."

I look at Reed. His eyes are boring into mine from behind Zane.

I give him a questioning look.

"Zane?! Can you help me please?" Daphne pleads.

"Be right there! Let me know if you need anything, ok?" He says, looking into my eyes.

"I will."

He takes off.

I look back to Reed. He lowers his eyes and walks away.

※

Thankfully, the rest of the hike goes smoothly.

When we get back to the castle, Zane says his goodbyes to Kya and Daphne. I hold back a laugh as I see Daphne's brown stained butt walk off. He turns his attention to me.

"I hope you enjoyed yourself, despite the, uh, incident." He rubs his hand through his hair. It's cute.

I chuckle, which seems to put him at ease. "I really did. Thank you for such a fun day."

"You're welcome." He grabs my hand and plants a kiss on the back of it. "See you soon."

I give him a small curtsy.

I go to the infirmary, grab a first aid kit, and start heading back to my room.

Reed pops up alongside of me.

"You seemed to really enjoy yourself today." His voice carries a clipped tone.

I look at him. "I did." I eye him suspiciously.

"Good."

"It is good." I answer, clipping back. "What's the problem, Reed?"

"Nothing. I am just glad you enjoyed your time with Zane today."

"You don't sound like it, and good! That's kind of why I am here."

"It is."

"So why are we having this conversation?!"

"I just had to let you know how happy I am that you seem to be catching his eye more and more. Maybe you will get that fairytale ending that all girls want."

We arrive at my door, but before I can reply, he's going back the way we came.

Furious, I enter my room and slam the door.

I pace back and forth in my room, replaying the stupid scene that just transpired.

*No!*

I was not about to let him have the last word.

I open my door angrily and am met with Reed's face, looking at me in a way that I have never seen before.

Before I can say anything, he grabs my face and presses a hard, wanting kiss on my lips. I grab his shirt and pull him into my room.

He shuts the door and pins me between the door and his body. His hands slide down my back, keeping me pressed against him. I run my hands through his hair.

I breathe in his delicious scent. It's reminiscent of woods and spices.

My face is becoming raw as his stubble moves across my face, but I don't care.

We pull apart when we are breathless.

"I'm sorry," he says, looking at me with glossed over eyes.

"You should be."

"I am finding that I am a very jealous man."

I smile. "If it leads to things like this, I really don't mind."

He gives me that sexy smirk of his and chuckles low, making my heart beat even faster.

He kisses my forehead and opens my door. He gives me one last glance and leaves.

I lean against the door and try, very unsuccessfully, to calm the pounding in my chest.

∘✿∘

Later that night, we dine with the Royal Family. I can't keep myself from glancing up at Reed. He looks incredibly handsome when he stands at attention. I love the way his muscular chest sticks out and how intense his eyes look. Reed's eyes catch mine.

*Busted.*

He gives me a small grin before looking away again. I look back down at my food, trying to hide my blush.

"We heard the hike was rather adventurous today," King Harden says, grinning.

All of us chuckle.

"To say the least," Kya says.

We all chuckle a little more.

"Well, we are glad that you are all ok," Queen Gabrielle says.

"Thank you, your majesty," I respond.

When dinner is finished, the king and queen exit, followed closely by Zane and Reed. Us girls leave last.

When I turn to go to the stairs that take me to my room, Reed steps in front of me.

"I trust you enjoyed dinner, Miss Moore?" He bows, taking my hand.

I raise an eyebrow at him. "I did …"

He lets go of my hand and walks away smiling. I feel something in my hand. I open my hand and see a folded piece of paper.

"Meet me in the library."

I swiftly make my way to the requested destination.

I find Reed sitting at a table with some wine and a couple of glasses.

He stands and grins when he sees me.

"I felt like you could use a drink after a slide like that."

I burst out laughing. "It was pretty bad, wasn't it?"

I take the seat opposite him.

He fills the cups and hands me one.

"Are you doing ok?" he asks.

"I am. After getting the scrapes cleaned and bandaged up, I hardly feel them."

"Good. I was worried that you might have sprained something."

"Nope. I am a tough girl."

He looks at me. "Yes, you are."

I look down into my glass.

"Isn't Zane going to notice you are missing?"

"Nah, he is getting ready for bed right now. I don't have to help with that, thank goodness."

"Oh, ok."

We sip in silence for a few minutes.

"I bet you were holding back a laugh watching us go down that hill."

He chuckles. "Maybe. Especially once I knew you were ok, and I saw Daphne's dirty backside."

I laugh. "Yeah, that *was* pretty funny. Seriously, it is not smart to wear white on a hike."

"No, it's not" Reed pauses. "You looked very pretty today."

I look at him, smiling. "Thank you."

He tips his head in a small bow.

We sit in comfortable silence as we finish our drinks.

"Well, I should probably head up to Zane's room. He wanted to talk to me about something."

"Ok. Thank you for the drink."

"You're welcome."

We both stand up and walk to the doors where we pause.

"Goodnight, Char."

I look up at him in surprise as he kisses my forehead.

He looks shocked. "I am sorry! Am I allowed to call you that?"

I smile. "Yes. I have never heard you say it before, so it just caught me off guard."

"But you're ok with it?"

"I like it very much."

He kisses me on the lips this time.

"Goodnight, Reed."

# Chapter 10

*Reed*

Zane is asking me what I think about each of the girls.

"Daphne is beautiful, but highly self-centered."

He nods in agreement.

"Kya is beautiful as well and has the sweetness to compliment that."

He grins and looks to the ground, smiling.

"As you know, Jazzie is out of the running."

He scratches the back of his head, no doubt remembering what went down in Estar.

"And Chartreuse?" I zone out on the wall behind Zane. "She is smart, selfless, and ornery as hell." I smile to myself.

"And what about her beauty?"

"She is the most beautiful of them all."

I look at Zane and see he is staring at me with an eyebrow raised.

I clear my throat. "My votes are for Kya and Chartreuse." Saying that makes my heart hurt. I don't want Zane to choose Char. I want him to choose Kya, so Char is free for me to pursue her. I want her for myself.

I want her face to be the one that I roll over and see every morning. I want her strong personality to be the one to square me off in an argument. I want to build her a large library that she can get lost in. I want to see her eyes when I look at my future children.

Despite what I want, I will not sabotage my best friend's chance at happiness, and quite possibly, hers. I will let things play out and hope, pray, no, *beg* God that he doesn't choose her and that she chooses me back.

# Chapter 11

*Chartreuse*

The next morning, I am walking around my room, getting ready for the day when I see a piece of paper on the floor, right next to my door.

I open it up and read: "Meet me at the 'sweet' bench. Reed."

I can't help but smile.

I hurry and finish getting ready then make my way there.

I exit out the servant doors and see a small picnic breakfast laid on the grass. When he sees me arrive, he gets up, and gives me a kiss.

"Good morning."

"Good morning. This looks delicious."

"Thank you. As you know, I put a lot of effort into stealing all of this from the kitchen."

"I know and I very much appreciate it."

We both grin and sit down. He has stolen for us scrambled eggs, bacon, toast, and fresh squeezed orange juice. We dig in.

"The King and Queen were going to announce it at breakfast this morning, but since I stole you away from that I figured that I should tell you."

I stare at him with a mouth full of food.

"There is going to be another ball tomorrow, to celebrate — I don't even know. You know how royals throw balls for everything."

I chuckle.

"Anyways, I figured you'd want to know."

"I would've. Thank you."

He smiles.

"You're going to be there, right?" I ask.

"As always."

I take a breath. "May I have a dance with you?"

He stops chewing and stares at me. "How in the world are we going to be able to do that in front of everyone, especially Zane?"

I shrug. "I know you'll figure something out."

He gives me a mischievous smile. "I will."

⚜

I stare at the three dresses that I brought with me. The dark blue one is out since I already wore that one, but I can't make up my mind which one to wear.

An idea hits me. I leave my room and search the castle for Reed. I find him standing outside one of the meeting rooms.

"Reed?" I whisper loudly around the corner to him.

"Char?"

"Yes. What's your favorite color?"

A pause. "What?"

"What's your favorite color?"

"Green. Why?"

"No reason."

"Knowing you, there's a reason."

"It's not a reason you need to know right now."

He's silent.

I peek around the corner and see him looking my way with an eyebrow raised.

"You'll know soon enough."

"Ok ..."

The meeting doors start to open. I duck back around the corner and head back to my room. I know exactly which dress I am going to wear.

⚜

Elise is as excited as I am while I get ready.

"Prince Zane is not going to be able to keep his eyes off of you!"

"Yes ... Zane." I smile knowingly to myself.

I put on the dress that I picked out for Reed. It is a satin, emerald green, high-low dress with spaghetti straps. I put on some matching pumps. I curl my hair then put it into a loose side braid. I look in the mirror and picture what Reed's face will look like when he sees me. It gets my heart beating faster.

"Wish me luck!"

"You don't need any luck, miss." She smiles.

"Thanks Elise." I give her a hug then head out into the hallway.

The music gets louder and louder as I approach the ballroom. I look inside. There are not as many people as there was for Zane's ball, but there is still a significant amount. I do *not* want to be heralded in again, so I find a side door and sneak in.

I scan the room for Reed. I find him standing next to the dais.

I wind my way through the crowd, keeping my eyes on him. When I am about ten feet in front of him, he catches sight of me.

His eyes go wide as his eyes roam down my outfit. When his eyes meet mine again, he gives me one of his sexy smirks. I give him a curtsy and he bows in return. I take a step toward him.

"Chartreuse, you look stunning tonight!"

I turn and see Zane. I give him a smile. "Thank you, Zane." I curtsy to him now.

"Would you honor me with this dance?"

83

"Absolutely." I take his outstretched hand.

We start gliding around the room. I steal glances at Reed as often as I can without alerting Zane. Every time I see Reed, he is looking right back at me.

"We are about halfway through your ladies' stay here. What do you think about that?"

I snap my attention back to him. "The time has definitely flown by. How about you?"

"Same."

"Any idea who you'll pick? If you're able to share that with me?"

"It's fine." He smiles. "I have some ideas, yes."

"Will the last two weeks come in handy?"

"Most assuredly."

The song winds down.

"I wish you an easy choice." I curtsy.

"Thank you." He bows back.

I turn back to where Reed was standing, but he is no longer there. I search the room as I walk around. I am not seeing him anywhere.

I feel someone grab my arm. I'm relieved when I turn and see Reed.

He holds his arm out and I weave mine through it. He leads me out through some double doors that take us to the gardens.

We reach a secluded area, deep in the maze that obstructs the view from the palace, but not the music.

Reed turns towards me taking my right hand. I place my left arm on his other am which wraps around my waist.

"So … this is why."

I smirk. "Do you like it?"

"I love it. I have never liked my favorite color as much as I do tonight."

He spins me out and brings me back in.

"You look very handsome tonight, in your full get up, very regal."

"Thank you."

We finish the rest of the song in silence. Another one starts up, but he doesn't let me go.

"You know, you are the only one I was looking forward to dancing with tonight," I say.

"Really? Even over Zane?"

I smile. "Even over Zane. While I was dancing with him, I was still looking at you when I could."

He pulls me close, his eyes fixed on mine. They seem to hide a mixture of emotions.

I place a kiss on his lips. Immediately, he stops dancing, pulls me closer with his arm, and places his other hand in my hair. He pulls back and leans his forehead on mine.

"I can never get enough of you, Char," he says.

"Good, because I can't get enough of you either."

He pulls me into another kiss.

"Reed?" It sounds like Zane.

Reed pulls back and groans. "Duty calls." He moves his hand to my face and rubs my cheek.

I smile, sadly. "I know."

He kisses my forehead and heads back to the castle.

To avoid raising suspicion, I wait a few minutes, then follow suit; but I don't return to the ball. Instead, I head back to my room.

"Back so soon?" Elise asks, shocked.

"Yes, I am afraid."

"Anything wrong?"

"No. I just already got to see who I wanted to see." I smile.

"Was it what you were expecting?"

"All that and more."

She smiles, content with my answer. "Would you like me to help you get ready for bed?"

"No, thank you. I can manage."

"Ok. Goodnight, miss."

"Goodnight."

I collapse onto my bed, still dressed in my gown and all. I stare at the ceiling until sleep finally succumbs me, hours later.

# Chapter 12

I wake up to another note having been slid under my door. I am smiling before I even open it.

"Meet me in the grove to the side of the castle. Reed."

I quickly throw myself together and make my way through the castle and out our usual servant door. I cross the grass and enter the collection of trees.

"Reed?"

No answer. I continue further in.

I come upon a small area without any trees, only grass. I see Reed on the other side.

After checking to make sure no one else is around, we walk into the clearing. I can't keep a smile from off my face. Meeting up with Reed never gets old.

When we reach other, we wrap our arms around each other and connect with heated kisses.

After a few minutes of being lost in each other's arms, Reed pulls away, with a quiet "Char," and looks at me with sad eyes. *Very* sad eyes. I don't like it.

I look at him, concern creeping across my face.

"What's wrong, Reed?"

He searches my face and takes a deep breath but doesn't say anything.

"You're scaring me."

"I — *We* — can't keep doing this. I mean, I want to, I am loving it, but it isn't fair to Zane, or to you."

I take a step back. "What do you mean?"

He takes another deep breath. "You came here for Zane, and I have been selfishly taking your attention away from him. It isn't right."

*No, Reed, please.*

"I am going to step back and let you pursue him, like you're supposed to, without confusion and without guilt." He looks down.

I understand what he is saying, but — "What if it's not what I want? What if *he's* not who I want? What if I want you?"

He looks back up at me. His eyes are wet.

"Then, if you are not meant to be with Zane, I will be waiting."

*This can't be it.*

I go to protest some more. "But —"

Reed takes a step back, bows, and says, "Until the next time, Miss Moore."

I feel my heart shatter into a million pieces. He doesn't look at me again. I watch him walk away and disappear back into the trees.

I collapse to the ground, my heartache overtaking me. The tears fall. Gasping sounds, escape my lips. Reed is gone and I can't do anything to stop it. He won't let anything stop it.

# Chapter 13

*Reed*

That was the hardest thing I have ever done. Saying those words. Seeing the hurt in her eyes. Walking away.

I push over a chair.

I hate myself for it, but she came here for Zane. I have been stealing her attention away from the man that could bring her happiness.

I throw a glass against the wall, shattering it.

I have been sabotaging Zane's chance at getting to know the wonderful Chartreuse Moore.

I collapse onto the floor.

The way her hair rivals the magnificence of the sun. The way her eyes see deep into my soul. The way her soft, sensual lips feel against mine. The harmonious sound of her laugh. Her spectacular stubbornness that is, somehow, able to match mine. The way she makes life worth living, worth pursuing. I miss her.

It has only been two days, but they have been agonizing. Especially since she hasn't been around for those two days and knowing that I caused it.

It's the evening of the second night, and I find myself in front of her door. My hand raises up like I am about to knock. How badly I want to burst into her room, get on my knees, and beg her forgiveness. Screw the happiness she could find with Zane. I *know* I make her happy … I *think* I make her happy. Does she feel for me the same way I feel for her?

Am I the last face she sees at night and the first she sees when she wakes? When she's having a bad day, am I the one she wants to run and talk to? Does she have thoughts about me that cause her to blush and look away?

I lower my hand.

*Please, Char. Please choose me, want me, need me. I love you.*

I turn and make my way back to my room, where I know I will face another sleepless night.

# Chapter 14

*Chartreuse*

The past two days have been a whirlwind of emotion. First, I was devastated, depressed. I could not believe what happened. I cried until I couldn't cry anymore.

Then, I was angry. Who was *he* to make the choice for the both of us? I was a part of us too! He shouldn't get to make such a choice without my input.

Eventually, I understood what he was saying. I still was not happy with what happened, but I got it.

I finally decide to leave my room. I put on my sunglasses to hide my puffy eyes and make my way outside, to the poolside. I slump into a chair. The sun brings a little healing, but not much.

Daphne and Kya join me shortly after. I groan quietly. I really wanted to be alone.

"Hi, Chartreuse!" Kya greets.

"Hi, Kya."

I know she can tell something is wrong, but she leaves it be.

*Thank you.*

Daphne, on the other doesn't.

"Well, someone seems to be in a foul mood today."

"Don't start Daphne. I am really not in the mood."

"I can see that."

She can't see it through my glasses, but I glare at her.

She moves to stand in front of me. "Did Zane say something? I didn't see you after your dance with him."

"It has nothing to do with him."

She gives me an unsympathetic moan with a mock frown. "Poor Chartreuse."

"Leave me alone, Daphne." There is warning in my voice.

"Or what? Surely, you didn't think you had a chance with Zane, with someone like me around, did you?"

*That's it.*

I jump up from my lounge chair, and tackle Daphne backwards — straight into the pool.

We are pulling at each other in the water. I can hear shouting coming from the surface. Neither Daphne nor I pay it any attention. We struggle and paw at each other until we run out of breath.

Once we resurface, I yell, "What is your problem, Daphne?! What have I, or any of the other girls, done to you?!"

She stares at me.

"Huh?!"

"Nothing!" she shouts back.

I stare at her, waiting to hear more.

"I had expected to come here and easily nab Zane's attention and hold it. But —"

I glare at her.

"But, I came here and saw the competition, and it scared me."

My face softens a little.

"Getting nasty is the only way I have ever dealt with competition."

I give her an understanding look.

"I am sorry," she says, looking down.

I sigh. "I am not saying what you have put me, *us*, through is acceptable, but it's ok. As long as you back off."

She looks up at me and nods.

I make my way to the ladder and hold my hand out to her. She grabs it.

After I pull her up, I turn around and go back inside. I need to find Zane.

⸎

I find him in the office, looking over some papers, with Reed not far away.

*Of course.*

I pause for a moment, thinking of a way to talk to Zane without Reed knowing. It's not possible. He will either follow us because it seems suspicious, or I have to outright ask for Zane's presence.

*Here goes nothing.*

I enter the room. "Zane?"

They both look to me. "Yes?! What can I do for you Chartreuse?" He smiles.

"I was hoping for a moment of your time — alone."

I see Reed furrow his brows. I look back to Zane.

"Absolutely. Reed? Would you excuse us please?"

Reed bows and makes his way out of the room. I can't look at him. I look at the ground as he passes, feeling his eyes on me. He shuts the door behind him.

Zane motions to a chair as he takes the one opposite. "What can I do for you, Chartreuse?"

How do you tell someone you are not interested in them? Then tell them you have feelings for their *best friend*?!

I take a deep breath. "I don't feel it's fair for me to continue to take up your time and draw any attention you may have for other ladies anymore."

He tips his head and looks at me with understanding eyes.

"I am afraid that I do not have feelings for you in the way that you need in a future queen and wife." I look into my lap.

There is silence. I look up.

His eyes are still kind, and he has a sad smile on his face. "You know? I was wondering that."

"I am so sorry."

"Don't be. There is enough heartache in this world without adding a loveless marriage to the mix." He takes my hands in his. "May I ask if there is anyone else who holds your heart?"

I stare at him a moment. "There is."

"May I ask who?"

I breathe out. "Reed."

He breaks out into a big smile. "That is great to hear."

*What?*

"What?"

He leans back in his chair. "Let me just say that Reed reciprocates your feelings."

My heart skips a beat then strains. "I thought so too, until he ended things with me a couple of days ago."

He sits up straight. "What? Why?"

"He said it wasn't good of him to be in the way of any possible happiness that you and I would have found with each other. That I came here for you and that he was backing out."

He rubs his hand over his face. "Oh Reed."

We sit in a silence for moment.

Zane stands. "Well, we have to fix this, don't we?"

"How are we going to do that?"

"With you backing out, my choice of wife is now clear, so there is no longer a need for you ladies being here."

"Ok …"

"We can end this vying for my hand and hold the announcement celebration early."

I stare at him, thinking I know where he is going.

"I can talk to Reed and let him know that he will be free to pursue you. He can't argue with me because I will have already chosen a wife."

A smile breaks across my face. "That is brilliant, Zane!" I stand and hug him. "Thank you so much!"

He hugs me. "Absolutely."

"When are you wanting to do this?"

"I was thinking tomorrow?"

"Perfect."

"We were planning on doing a masquerade. You know, *unmasking* my future wife?"

"I love it."

"I will announce this at dinner tonight."

"Sounds great." I hug him again.

I turn to leave. When my hand touches the doorknob, he asks, "Chartreuse?"

I look back at him. "Yes?"

"If Reed hadn't of been here, would you have fallen for me?"

I give him a big smile. "Most definitely."

He returns the smile.

I walk out. Reed is standing against the wall across the hall. His eyes meet mine.

I can't hide the smile that spreads across my face. I can't wait until tomorrow.

He gives me a small bow.

*If only you knew. But you will. Soon enough.*

# Chapter 15

Thankfully, my last dress works well for a masquerade. It's a black ballgown with a sweetheart neckline, that goes out into a puffy skirt. Elise curls my hair and leaves it down. It's a nice contrast to the black dress and mask that I place over my eyes. It covers my forehead and nose with feathers coming out from the top. I finish with bright red lipstick.

"You look incredible," Elise says, holding her hands under her chin.

"Thank you. I kind of want to blow him away." I put my hands on my nervous stomach.

"You definitely will."

I hug her and make my way to the ballroom.

Much like the first party, it is swarming with people. Except, this time, it looks like an elegant zoo with all of the covered faces and various colors swirling around the room.

I scan the room for Reed, but I don't find him.

I look for Zane. He is easy to find. He is dressed like a powerful lion. I walk up to him. "Have you seen Reed?"

"I have not." He pauses. "You look beautiful, by the way."

"Thank you. You look good too."

"Thank you." We both search around the room again.

"Maybe he just stepped out for a moment. I will give it another minute and then make the announcement."

"Ok." I wipe my sweaty, nervous hands on my dress. "Have you talked with your choice and let her know yet?"

He looks right at Kya, who is along the wall, and replies, "Yes." He has a sweet smile on his face. She catches his gaze and returns it.

*Precious.*

"I am going to go get a drink. Good luck, Zane."

"Thank you."

I find a waiter with a tray, swipe a glass of champagne, and down it in one gulp.

"If I may have everyone's attention," Zane announces to the room.

I look around and still don't see Reed.

"As you all know, four beautiful ladies came here, vying for my hand. I am happy to announce, that I have made my decision." The room stills.

"I would like to ask Lady Kya Hale to join me." He holds out his hand.

She quickly finds her way up to him and takes it.

"Everyone, let's give a proper cheer for Kya Hale, my fiancé, and future Queen of Uspia." The room erupts into deafening cheers. They share a sweet kiss which makes the cheers even louder.

I give another glance around the room, but still don't see Reed.

*Where has he gone?*

The music starts up again and Zane finds me, hand in hand with Kya.

"Congratulations!" I give Kya a hug.

"Thank you so much!"

"So ... Where is it?"

She holds out her hand and on her ring finger, is a large diamond ring.

"It's beautiful!"

"Beautiful ring for a beautiful woman." Zane chimes in. They look at each other.

"I still don't see Reed. Do you know where he would be?" I ask.

"I think I may. I'll be right back."

I look at Kya. "How are you feeling?"

"Like I could fly." She is all grins.

I chuckle. "I am sure."

"I really can't believe that he chose me."

I smile. "I can."

"Thank you."

I look around the room again. Still no Reed. However, I see Daphne, standing against the wall, looking out at everyone. I want to see how she is holding up not being picked by Prince Zane, so I make my way over.

"Hey, Daphne." I offer a small smile.

"Hey, Chartreuse." She answers sadly.

"How are you doing?"

She shrugs. "I am ok, considering the circumstances." She nods towards Kya.

"I am sorry."

"Don't be. I'll be fine. I'm a tough girl." She smiles, but it doesn't quite reach her eyes.

I wrap my arms around her and chuckle. "I know, believe me."

She hugs me back, laughing. I pull back.

"Well, I hope you are still able to enjoy the festivities of the masquerade."

She scoffs. "Of course! I love dancing. No better way to get over a handsome prince than by dancing with a bunch of handsome strangers."

"I bet." We stand in silence for a moment. "I'll see you around, Daphne."

"See you."

I start making my way back to Kya. Zane comes out of nowhere, breathless.

"I told Reed ... What you said ... He ran out ..."

"What?! Which way did he go?!"

Zane points to the main ballroom doors. "Out the front doors."

I grab my skirt and take off running.

I make it to the doors and out onto the front steps of the castle. I see him getting into a waiting car.

"Reed!"

He barely turns arounds to catch a quick glimpse of me. "I'm sorry ma'am. I have something I need to do."

I rip off my mask. "Reed, you idiot!"

He stops and gets out of the car. He has his sexy, crooked smile plastered on his face. "You're never going to let me forget this, are you?"

"Never." I am grinning ear to ear. We start to slowly walk towards each other.

He looks me up and down. "You look incredible in that dress."

"Thank you. Where were you?"

"I couldn't be there, just in case —" he pauses, "he said your name."

We stop just a few inches away from each other. His delicious, clean cologne fills my nose. He is searching my face.

He cups my face with his hand. "Zane told me what you said."

I can only nod my head. Tears threaten to fall.

He breaks out into a relieved smile. "I cannot believe this is happening."

"You *better* believe it."

"I love you, Char."

"I love you t—" His lips crash on mine before I can finish.

He pulls away. "I know." He strokes my cheek.

This time, I bring him to me. Kissing him hard. He picks me up and I wrap my arms around his neck.

After a minute, he sets me back down.

"So, where were you going so fast?" I ask, raising an eyebrow.

His sexy smirk is back. "Come with me."

The limo takes us to a jeweler's.

*No way.*

I look at Reed. "You're not one to wait, are you?"

"I was *not* going to waste my second chance." I take his out-stretched hand.

We walk into the store. Except for the jeweler behind the counter, we are the only ones there.

"Take your pick."

I snap my head to him. "No way."

He chuckles. "Way."

I smack him. I wander along all the glass counters, checking out every single one of them. I settle on a modest, single, square-cut diamond.

"Are you sure? You don't want something more elaborate?"

I shake my head. "I am a simple girl, remember?"

"I do." Reed points at my ring.

"Good choice." The jeweler says, handing it to Reed. He immediately drops down to one knee.

All air leaves my lungs.

"Char. I know I am *not* who you hoped to fall for, but I promise that I will spend my whole life showing you that your choice was not in vain. Will you marry me?"

"Of course I will."

He places the ring on my finger and picks me up, swinging me around as we kiss.

# Chapter 16

I wiggle my finger, watching the light dance off its new, shiny occupant. Reed takes my hand and places a kiss over the diamond.

"I'm glad you like it."

"I don't like it, I love it." I lean over and kiss him.

We are in the limo on our way to my home, to *officially* introduce him to them as my fiancé.

"Are you nervous?" I ask.

"Why would I be? Meeting the parents of my future wife when they know how we started out. And being the reason why their daughter didn't become queen. I am ecstatic." His reply is dripping with sarcasm.

I chuckle. "They will love you."

I lean my head on his shoulder and he leans his head on mine.

"Thank you for choosing me." He whispers.

"Thank you for wanting me."

He kisses the top of my head. "You are the first and only woman I have ever wanted."

*Butterflies.*

I wonder how long those will last? We haven't known each other for very long, so I am hoping they will stick around for a while. I quite enjoy the sensation.

We pull up to my house. My family is on the porch. This time,

Violet cannot contain herself and is bobbing up and down. I roll my eyes and smile.

I turn to Reed. "Ready?"

He nods and gets out. He walks around and opens my door for me. I take his hand.

Next to bobbing Violet is my mom, who is smiling widely. Next to her, is my dad, who has a look of indifference on his face. I feel Reed squeeze my hand. I squeeze it back.

We approach Violet first.

"Hello, Miss Violet," Reed addresses.

Violet blushes. "Hello, Reed."

I give my sister a hug.

"Nice to see you again, Mrs. Moore." Reed kisses my mother's hand.

"Nice to see you again, too." She curtsies.

My mother and I kiss each other's cheeks.

We stand in front of my dad. His expression has not changed.

"Nice to see you again, too, Mr. Moore." Reed holds out his hand. My dad doesn't take it.

I stop breathing.

"You're not the prince." My father states, flatly.

Reed's hand lowers. "You're right, sir. I plan on treating your daughter like a queen regardless."

My dad smiles at this and wraps Reed up in a hug. "Welcome to the family, son."

Reed releases my hand and hugs him back.

*Whew.*

I hug my dad next. As I pull away, my mom smacks him on the arm.

"Ow!" He whispers, looking at her. She gives him a stern look and he smiles.

We head inside. As we eat lunch, we catch my family up on

everything that happened after our stop here. They hang onto every word.

"Have you guys talked about the wedding at all?" My mom asks.

We look at each other. "We have." I say. "We are planning on something small and simple; secluded area, simple dress, and only family and close friends."

She beams.

"How about where you will be living?" My dad asks.

Reed answers this time. "Since I am a member of the royal guard, it makes sense for us to stay at the palace in Uspon." My dad smiles, but his eyes are sad.

"However —" I but in. "We will be making regular trips back to visit." I smile.

"Good."

⚘

We take off after dinner.

"See? That wasn't so bad." I say.

"It definitely went way better than I expected."

I wrap my arm through his and look out the window. Images flash across my mind: a white dress, messy beds, fights where neither wants to back down, children's faces, graying hair. I smile and lay back onto the seat, closing my eyes.

*Bring it on.*

This book was greatly inspired by the series "The Royal Romance" from Choices. Thank you so much for taking me to Cordonia and helping me find true love in unexpected places.